Hide, Don't Seek (A Why Choose Dark Romance)

Not-So Childish Games Duet Book 1

TRIS WYNTERS

Kayla Englert

Tris Wynters Publishing

Copyright © 2024 by Tris Wynters

All rights reserved. No part of this book may be reproduced in any manner whatsoever without written permission except in the case of brief quotations embodied in critical articles and reviews.

This book is a work of fiction. Any names, characters, companies, organizations, places, events, locales, and incidents are either used in a fictitious manner or are fictional. Any resemblance to actual persons, living or dead, actual companies or organizations, or actual events is purely coincidental.

For rights and permissions, please contact:
triswyntersbooklover23@gmail.com

First Printing, 2024
Editing and Proofreading By: Kayla Englert

CONTENTS

DEDICATION - vii
CONTENT & TRIGGER WARNINGS - xi
PLAYLIST - xv

~Chapter 1~
1

~Chapter 2~
13

~Chapter 3~
25

~Chapter 4~
34

~Chapter 5~
39

~Chapter 6~
49

~Chapter 7~
56

~Chapter 8~
64

~Chapter 9~
70

~Chapter 10~
73

~Chapter 11~
78

~Chapter 12~
88

~Chapter 13~
92

~Chapter 14~
99

~Chapter 15~
104

~Chapter 16~
114

~Chapter 17~
118

~Chapter 18~
127

~Chapter 19~
132

~Chapter 20~
137

~Chapter 21~
144

~Chapter 22~
148

~Chapter 23~
152

~Chapter 24~
156

~Chapter 25~
162

~Chapter 26~
171

~Chapter 27~
181

~Chapter 28~
186

~Chapter 29~
190

~Chapter 30~
204

~Chapter 31~
210

A NOTE FROM THE AUTHOR - 217
ALSO BY TRIS WYNTERS - 219

If masked mercenaries with piercings make you drool,
turn the page.

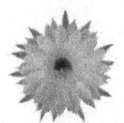

Good girl.

CONTENT & TRIGGER WARNINGS

This book is a reverse harem/ why choose. The female main character will have multiple love interests and will not have to choose between them.

In this book, the male characters focus most of their attention on the female. However, two of them are in a relationship and do have brief, dirty innuendos.

This is a work of fiction that contains dark elements meant for mature readers only.

Depictions of past and current physical and sexual assault are portrayed in this book. Additionally, the characters have their own way of dealing with their trauma.

This book also discusses BDSM practices, which may make some readers uncomfortable. First and foremost, please note that consent is the main focus; as it should be.

A list of trigger warnings can be found on the next page. If you have additional questions or concerns, please reach out to triswyntersboolover23@gmail.com

Past Memories

Coercion
Physical Assault
SA by Boss
SA by Friend
CSA by Family Member
Bullying
Self-Harm
Witness of Murder

Present Story

Masked Men
Gagging
Bondage
CNC
Primal Play
Edging
Squirting
Physical and Sexual Assault
Eye-Gouging
Torture
Light Stalking
Vigilante Shit
Depression
Self-Harm
Panic Attacks
Flashbacks
Suicidal Ideation
Inability to orgasm- Medical/Mental
Murder

xiv ~ Content & Trigger Warnings

PLAYLIST

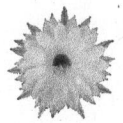 

Boy Problems by Aston
Dance, Dance by Fall Out Boy
Bad Idea, Right? by Olivia Rodrigo
I Stand Alone by Godsmack
Put Your Records On by Corinne Bailey Rae
Vampire by Olivia Rodrigo
I'm Tired by Labrinth and Zendaya
Hate Me by Blue October
Closer by Nine Inch Nails
Birthday Sex by Jeremih
Wicked Games by The Weeknd
Wildest Dreams by Taylor Swift
Lust for Life by Lana Del Rey

HIDE, DON'T SEEK (A WHY CHOOSE DARK ROMANCE)

~CHAPTER 1~

My lungs are on fire and my breaths are sawing in and out of my chest at an alarming rate. The air is thick with humidity and the sun is just about to set. Not that I can see much as I sprint through the forest. With the various Oak trees and the gorgeous Loblolly Pine canopy looming over me, this forest is creepy as shit. But the man behind me...

My foot catches on an exposed tree root. The ground quickly rises to meet me and I crash into it with an *oomph*. I swallow down the pain splintering through my hands, knees, and right ankle. I don't have time to brush away the rocky debris or examine them for damage. I have to go *now*.

Without a second thought, I push myself up, untangle my ankle from the dang root, and keep running. My breaths are coming out in harsh pants as I try to regain my bearings and determine which way to go.

A twig snaps from somewhere behind me, alerting me of just how close he is. *Too close. Fork.*

I turn towards the left and sprint through the wooded area; ducking and dodging a mixture of Post Oak and Red Maple trees with low limbs that appear to be reaching out for me. I am way too fat to be running like this. My heart is crashing against my ribs and I'm pretty sure it's going to pump right out of my chest. *Holy hell. I'm going to die.*

Up ahead, I notice a small space beneath a trail bridge. *Thank God for the current drought.* I know I need to take a break to get my heart rate under control, and that's the best opportunity for now.

I pump my arms as my feet carry me across the ground. Hope spurs in my chest at the thought of hiding out for a little bit.

Just then, a painful stitch on my left side causes me to double over in pain. *Schnitzel.*

"Come out, come out, wherever you are..." his deep, masked voice taunts me; seeming to surround me on all sides. Fear shoots down my spine and into my toes.

Knowing I need to hide, and fast, I limply jog the last few feet to the edge of the bridge. It's really steep on this side but the underbrush of the forest should help hide me. Lowering my upper body a little, I start to carefully slide my feet down the rocky slope. Just as I reach out for the lowest beam of the bridge so I can use it to help steady myself on my way down, a huge, meaty hand grabs around my bicep. *How the hell did I not hear him?*

I scream out in terror as he yanks me toward him. Stumbling over my feet, I'm suddenly slammed against a nearby tree; the bark cutting into my back through my shirt. Faster than I can blink, he releases his hold on my bicep, trapping me against the tree with his whole body. Before I can do anything, his hand clasps around my wrist and lifts it above my head; pinning it to the tree.

"Noooo!" I cry out. Using my other hand, I hit him in the shoulder and arm, trying to get him to let me down. His biceps barely flinch under his black, short-sleeve tee. I don't even try to hit his chest as it's covered by a tactical vest decked out with more ammo and knives than I thought possible.

With a low growl, his other hand wraps around my flailing wrist and pins it to the tree. His fingers maneuver quickly and I'm surprised to realize that both of my wrists are now firmly in one of his huge hands. His large, rough fingers completely engulf them and lock them securely in place. I try to kick out, my adrenaline boosting into overdrive, but he's so dang close to my body that I don't land a single kick.

"Stop!" His command whips out through the darkening forest. My body freezes as he pushes up against me; the weight of his armored vest pressing into my chest.

He stands at least a head taller than me. His eyes look hazel in the dark and are boring into mine with need and excitement. They're accentuated because his mouth is covered by one of those creepy half-skull masks that only cover the bottom half of his face. A plain, black beanie sits atop his head and is pulled all the way down to his brows.

My whole body thrums with adrenaline as he leans his head closer, my boobs smashing against his vest as he whispers, "I told you I'd catch you."

I lean forward and growl, "Get. The fork. Off of me," before snapping my teeth in his direction.

He barely misses my teeth as he flinches back with a deep, throaty chuckle. "Oh, baby girl," he groans out. "I like you feisty." His free hand collars my throat and shock jolts through me as I feel the smooth coolness of leather gloves. I can feel his thumb and pointer fingers pressing on my carotid arteries and the middle of his palm just barely grazes the front of my neck. My heart rate picks up and I begin to feel dizzy.

I try to wriggle out of his grip but it only tightens. My breasts brush roughly over his vest as I squirm in his arms. My stupid body betrays me and my nipples stiffen into taut peaks.

Tilting his head, he assesses me. The sun disappearing from the sky makes his whole aura even more terrifying. The thin sliver of skin shown between the two pieces of black cloth lets me see his eyes crinkle at the corners, signaling that he's smiling.

A sob breaks loose from my throat as fear strangles me. "P-please," I beg, as tears fall down my cheek.

"Awww, you beg so pretty," he coos sardonically. Releasing my throat, he grabs onto the bottom of the mask lying around his neck. He lifts it, fast enough that I don't get to see anything before he bends down to my jaw. My body freezes and my eyes grow wide as I feel his tongue dart out, licking a path from my jaw to just above my cheek. His soft beard tickles me as it follows the path of his tongue. *Is that a tongue piercing?*

Just as my thought finishes, he quickly pulls his mask back down his neck. "Mmm," he groans huskily. "Your tears taste like heaven."

I whimper, trembling uncontrollably. Liquid heat pools in my panties as my body gets its wires crossed.

His deep voice washes over me like honey when he grumbles, "Now, are you going to be a good girl for me, or do I need to gag you?"

"Wh-what?" I squeal. "No, please. No!" I begin thrashing my body again, desperately hoping to get away.

His disappointed "Tsk-Tsk," brings my attention back to him. *He's tsking me like a child?! What the hell?*

"That wasn't the answer I was hoping for," he sighs condescendingly. "Nonetheless, you've made your choice." He sounds like a father who's upset that his child chose to play video games instead of doing her chores.

"What choi-" My question is cut off abruptly as the sound of metal cuffs jingle through the air. The cold metal bites into my right wrist, and I whip my head up just in time to see him quickly yank the connecting chain over a wide, low branch. "No!" I scream, trying to wrench my other hand away. His body presses impossibly harder into mine as he snaps the cuffs on my other wrist. That's when I realize that he's cuffed me to a branch that curves upwards, making it impossible for me to scoot off of it. *Crap on a cracker!*

"Please, please, please. Let me go. Please." My breath is coming out in heavier pants as he steps back to assess his handiwork. Tilting his head like a creepy soldier of death, he hums in the back of his throat, then steps forward.

"No! Please don't do this. Stooppppl!" I scream and struggle as I kick out; pretty sure I'm moments away from passing out. His large, gloved hand cups over my mouth, silencing my screams.

"Now, now. You've made your choice. I'm just gunna..." With his free hand, he lifts the mask off of his neck once more and I watch as he takes a fingertip of the glove into his mouth. Pinching it between his teeth, he deftly removes the glove. The tiny sliver of light left in the forest shows me an inky patch on his hand. A tattoo. But it's too dark to really see it.

Uncovering my mouth, he quickly shoves his now-free glove in before pulling out some duct tape. *What in the actual forkballs?* A loud rip echoes through the forest as he takes a piece and covers the glove with it; securing it to my face.

Tears are flooding my face and I'm shaking my head with so much vigor that I'm making myself dizzy.

Once he's finished, he slides his hand into my sweaty hair and yanks my head towards his; squeezing the roots at the top of my neck. "That's better. Don't you think?"

His mouth is still exposed from pulling up the mask and I feel the warmth of his breath tickle my face. He's now close enough that I can see and feel his thick beard against my neck but it's too dark to tell the color or length.

I'm feeling floaty and having a hard time breathing with the wad of leather hanging out in my mouth.

Pressing his body against mine, his hands begin to roam my body; squeezing my hips, trailing up my ribcage, cupping my breasts. A low moan escapes his throat as he continues his perusal.

"I love this shirt. So cute, so pretty, so *many* buttons." And with that, he rips my favorite baby blue, flowy button-up right down the middle. Buttons litter the forest floor and the cool, damp air whips across my chest. My twilight-colored tee-shirt bra is now on full display for this man, and I desperately shift, wishing I could cover up.

I consider snapping twice but the lust coursing through my body, and knowing it's probably too dark for him to really see anything, has me dismissing the idea.

He takes off his other glove, tossing it on the ground, and uses both hands to flip the cups of my bra down, exposing my breasts to him. The cool evening air causes them to pebble and he groans appreciatively. "Fucking perfect," he whispers right before he gropes them both. He leans in and sucks one of them right into his mouth. A muffled scream rips from my throat as he bites down enough to cause sparks of pain to shoot down to my clit.

He pops off one nipple and languidly kisses down my squishy belly. I cringe and flinch inward, desperately trying to suck in my flabby belly. His wide shoulders begin to lower with his body before he drops to his knees in front of me. Grasping my ass, he pulls my jean-covered crotch right into his nose and inhales deeply. My eyes widen with fear and arousal because, apparently, I'm jacked in the head, and I feel even more wetness pool in my panties.

Without further ado, he quickly unbuttons my jeans and rips the zipper down so fast that it takes a moment for my brain to process. My adrenaline ramps up as my brain processes what's happening. Squirming, closing my eyes, trying to bend down; I do everything I can to close myself off from this man, but nothing works.

A loud, sharp smack lands on my ass, and a yelp barely penetrates the air. "Mine," he growls low in warning.

He wastes no more time, sliding my jeans down to my ankles, bringing my twilight-colored thong with them. Now, my feet are pinned and I can't even try to kick out. My mind rushes through some kind of escape plan as darkness closes in around us.

Then, a warm wet tongue meets my slit and runs all the way up. "Delicious," he groans looking up at me. "Are you wet for me? Does having you all tied up and at my mercy turn you on?"

I scream through the glove, shaking my head violently, and try to shift away from him. "Awww. You sure?" he asks teasingly. Then one of his thick fingers slides through my most intimate area; once, twice, before he brings them to his mouth and sucks them clean. "Your lies are tasty." I groan and bump my head back against the tree, hating my stupid body for giving me away.

My heart rate doubles as anticipation tries to kill me. Two thick digits open me up wide, and I feel my cheeks heat in embarrassment over being so exposed. I can't even bring myself to look down at him as fear, shame, and arousal, all fight through my body for dominance.

And then, his tongue pokes out and flicks my needy little clit and I have to fight back a moan. I feel him shift as he takes one hand, spins it upside down, and spreads his fingers wide, opening me up to him fully. I fail to suppress the violent shiver that ripples through my body as I feel the air whip across my naughty bits.

His other hand makes its way from my clit, to my entrance and back up, before circling my clit with gentle, barely there pressure. After the third, deliberate pass, I'm equal parts ashamed and wanton, causing me to sob loudly through the leather glove.

"Sshhhh, it's ok. I'll take care of this needy little cunt." His words drip with sex and dominance, and my pussy clenches painfully.

One of his strong fingers slams right into me and I cry out at the intrusion. Before I can even adjust, he circles my clit with his tongue, slides his finger out of me, then pushes two in. My knees buckle at the sensations and the cuffs cut into my wrists as I writhe in the air before him.

Licking, teasing, sucking, he devours my clit like a man starved for food. Meanwhile, his fingers pump in and out of me, thrusting in a harmonic rhythm with the patterns of his tongue. I feel his fingers curl into me, hitting that little rough spot deep inside, and I feel an orgasm starting to build. The pressure is intense, but I fight it. One: because I don't have them often, and two: because I don't want this man to know how he's affecting me.

A hard swat to my exposed pussy startles me, and I shriek, the noise muffled by the leather glove. His low, menacing growl is barely heard over my whimpering sobs and the beating of my heart. "You *will* cum for me. Do you understand?"

I shake my head, fighting my body, fighting him. "Oh really? You think you can hold back from me?" He snarks.

A broken " Screw you" is trapped behind my covered mouth, but I can tell the insult lands. His answering chuckle causes a shiver to run down my spine and makes my nerves even more on edge. "Oh, I will. Don't worry about that."

The moment he finishes speaking, he goes back to attacking my clit with an intensity I've never experienced before. The metal barbell in his tongue sends lightning through my clit with each swirl. I don't know what the hell he's doing but the mixture of his tongue's ministrations, paired with the rough thrusting of his fingers pressing on my G spot, sends me spiraling higher.

"Cum for me, dirty girl," he purrs right before sucking my clit into his mouth.

And. I. Lose it.

My whole body shakes as my orgasm crests and I hear the faint sounds of his fingers working through each gush.

"That's my girl. Good girl," he murmurs as he leisurely pumps his fingers in and out of me, helping to bring me down from the orgasm.

My body begins to sag, causing the metal cuffs to dig into my wrists. A whimper catches in my throat and I can feel the tears cascading down my cheeks.

He slowly rises to his full height, takes my jaw in his hand, and rips the duct tape from my mouth. I barely have time to wince before he's whipping the glove from my mouth and smashing his lips to mine. The taste of myself mixed with something cinnamon explodes on my tongue as he presses his tongue into my mouth. His tongue demands attention and obedience and, for some reason, I give it to him. The scratch of his very full beard sends tingles down my spine and I moan at the feeling.

Breaking the kiss, his chest brushes mine with each inhale. He reaches one hand up and quickly slides the mask back over his mouth, securing his beard underneath, before he reaches up and unlocks the cuffs.

My body is heavy and spent, so I immediately start to collapse, but he catches me with one bulging arm around the waist before I can hit the ground. However, he doesn't give me time to process the relief or formulate a plan to run. His hand immediately finds my left wrist, steps behind me, and grabs my other wrist; bringing them together behind my back and causing my chest to stretch out.

One giant paw now holds both of my wrists and he presses up against me. I can feel his hard length pressing into my back and my stupid pussy clenches with a needy ache. *Hussy.*

Leaning in, he gruffly whispers, "On your knees, baby girl."

He doesn't give me a chance to protest as his knee roughly collides with the back of mine, causing it to buckle under the pressure. My knees collide with the rough ground and I scream out. I'm pretty sure a stick just became one with my shin. My pants are still snug around my ankles, preventing me from moving much as he leans over me, forcing my body to lean forward until my head is parallel to the forest floor.

The metal clanking of a buckle being loosened, quickly followed by his zipper zinging open, causes me to widen my eyes. Tremors wrack my body and I begin to shimmy my shoulders, trying to free myself from his grip.

A sharp sting sparks across my ass cheek, causing me to freeze. "Now, now, baby girl. No need to fight it."

Tears continue down my face and collect on the ground beneath me. I am well and truly overwhelmed as I mumble nonsensically, but he doesn't respond. Instead, the blunt tip of his hard cock prods my embarrassingly wet entrance. *Holy schnitzel, is that a piercing? Fork nuggets.*

Before I can take in another breath, his cock plunges deep inside me and I feel his balls slap my clit. Gasping loudly, tears blur my vision as my pussy stretches to accommodate his large size. And, *jeer desus. I'm pretty sure there's more than one piercing.*

"So. Fucking. Tight. So damn wet." He grits through the mask. Without another thought, he pulls out and slams back in, releasing a long, low groan.

"Fuck, you're squeezing me so good, baby girl." My eyes flutter closed as every nerve ending in my body lights on fire.

And then, he's moving.

Thrust after thrust he pummels my pussy like it personally wronged him. His balls tap my clit with each thrust and our thighs clap loudly through the dark forest. I can feel my body gripping around him with every pull and cheering in ecstasy with every push. His left hand never leaves my wrists but his right hand makes its way in front of my body and slides down, prodding under my hood. A fleeting pressure from his fingers causes me to moan out as he continues to bruise every inch of my cervix.

A low moan leaves his mouth and he pulls my wrists back toward him, "Up, on your knees." He groans. Following the direction of his pull, I sit up on my knees which pushes his cock into a whole other neighborhood of pleasure.

"Goddamn. So good. You're so good," He rasps in my ear, the soft cotton of his mask brushing against my neck eliciting goosebumps to run down my body. "You're taking my dick like such a good girl. I knew you would. Oh G-" He breaks off on a pant and returns his fingers back to my clit, pressing in firm, rapid circles.

"Cum for me." I shake my head, already spent from one orgasm and trying my damnedest to hold out.

"Wrong answer," He barks while slapping my pussy.

A guttural moan leaves my chest when his fingers return to my clit, immediately replacing the shock of the pain with overwhelming pleasure. His whole body vibrates as his pelvis smacks my ass with each punishing thrust.

"I. Said. Cum." He grits, then pinches my clit. My body betrays me by going off like a bottle rocket. I feel freaking *everything* as he continues strumming my clit like a guitar chord.

And. He doesn't. Stop.

My orgasm crests over the peak... then stalls. And stalls. And stalls.

My breath gets caught in my chest as my core clenches inward. Then, my whole body locks up as fireworks burst in front of my eyes. I barely register a groan but can't miss the undeniable emptiness that comes with him removing his cock while continuing to ruin my clit.

Suddenly, the spring in my core snaps. Gushes of liquid flood from my body, pooling between my knees and drenching the ground beneath me. My body starts to sag in exhaustion but his metal-filled dick slams into me again, causing me to whimper from over-sensitivity.

He slams in two more times before I feel him spill his entire load inside of me. My body shivers as his roar makes my nerve-endings tingle in appreciation and I really hope he doesn't notice.

~CHAPTER 2~

For just a brief moment, he holds me against his chest; our breathing syncing as we both come down from the high. His forehead rests against the back of my head as he gently slides his fingers down my wretched curves.

I feel myself tense as reality catches up with me and I start retreating back into myself.

Tugging a little, I signal for him to release my wrists. He slowly does, holding his other hand across my dreaded stomach so I don't fall face-first. Once satisfied that I'm stable, he moves his hand to join the other in massaging my wrists and hands, helping to get the circulation moving again.

My body is still trembling but I force myself to shift on my knees as they scream against the hard ground. After a few seconds, he releases my arms and I feel his heat disappear from behind me. The humid air mixes with the sweat on my skin and I'm silently thankful when a gentle breeze decides to blow under the canopy.

I hear the rustling of leaves and twigs as he cleans himself up and puts his cock back in his pants. Knowing I need to get out of here, I scramble to stand, momentarily forgetting that my pants are still around my ankles. I get caught up in them and start to pitch forward but his large, warm hand reaches out and saves me. "Woah there. Here, let me help you up. I also brought some supplies for aftercare..."

I'm already shaking my head as embarrassment and shame set in. Awkwardly, I shuffle out of his hold; bringing up my soaked jeans as I go. Once they're secured over most of my flab, I tightly wrap the remains of my shirt across my front and fold my arms. I don't bother with the dirt or debris right now. I'll rinse off in the shower before immersing myself in a bubble bath.

Turning towards him, I see that he's already put back together and he's assessing me with his head tilted to the side. I don't need pleasantries. I'm just the big girl he found on the app to explore fantasies with. One of hundreds, I'm sure, based on how *forking* amazing he was.

I thrust my hand out to pass him back his glove. Almost hesitantly, he reaches out and takes the glove. Though his expressions are mostly hidden under the mask, it appears that he isn't sure what to say now.

Clearing my throat, I dart my eyes around and smile gently. "Th-thank you, but, I don't need aftercare. Um-"

"Every sub needs aftercare," He says vehemently. I can tell he's scowling by the lines around his eyes and the dip of his beanie.

Shaking my head, I suck in a deep breath and put on my best smile. "I'm good. Promise."

We stand there awkwardly for a beat. Then, I smile again and move to turn away.

"Can I see you again?" His blurted question catches me completely off-guard and I know it shows all over my face.

"Uh, um, like, you want to play again? I mean, sure. If you really want to. But, you don't have to. It was...fun." I say with a shy smile and start backing away towards the bridge that will lead me to the parking lot.

I see his eyes pull down as if he's confused by my answer. "Of course, I want to see you again. But, it doesn't have to be a scene. We could..." He coughs and clears his throat, bringing his hand up to rub the back of his neck. "Like, have dinner or something."

"Wh-what?" I'm frozen in place as I try to figure out his real intentions.

"Well, we've been messaging on the app for a few weeks now and we know that, um, this type of stuff syncs up. I'd really like to hang out. Get to know you." He shrugs a shoulder innocently; like he's nervous about asking me. It's kinda cute, actually. *He's screwing with me. Or maybe this is his first time meeting someone on the app, and he thinks he has to offer more.*

"Um. I don't really have time for stuff like that. I know this was a scene for you and just a kink to explore. And, you don't have to worry about protecting my feelings; that's kind of what the app is for." I shrug with a half smile.

I'm not that girl. I'm not the one guys go after. I'm the good friend, the wing-woman, or the little sister. I am utterly ordinary and have more flab than guys like. Which is precisely why I searched dozens of apps before deciding that, the one E met through, fit my needs perfectly. Apparently, some guys like to explore plus-size kinks, without the embarrassing social norms. So, they get to play out a fantasy, and I get a release. Ok, a full release barely happens but, hey, sometimes a woman just wants to be touched and desired, dang it. *I got a full release today, though.*

Shaking my head to prevent myself from grinning like a fool, I quickly add, "Anyways, thank you, again. And, if you want to play again, let me know." I don't give him a chance to respond as I turn on my heel and make my way back through the forest. I don't need him feeding me any crap just to make himself feel better for living out a fantasy, then chunking deuce. Big girls may be great friends, but sometimes we need more than toys to play with. After all, that's the whole reason I joined the app.

I found the app a year ago and have matched with a couple of guys. They do full background checks on every member. Additionally, members have to post the location, date, and time into the app for the other person to consent to. This allows the site to have a paper trail in case something goes sideways. Plus, they require extensive medical checks before and after each meeting.

My rules are front-and-center on my profile bio so there's no confusion.

1. One of us has to wear a mask.
2. No kissing.
3. No real names.
4. No humiliation about my weight.
5. No sharing personal information outside of kink/scene ideas.

I cringe a little realizing that I let him kiss me. I was so lost in the euphoria of the orgasm and my reaction to his body was instantaneous. That man is dangerous in his own right. Tall, sexy, those dang arms, piercings, and tattoos. *Good gracious.* He's exactly the type of guy I'd fall hopelessly for and end up with my heart ripped to shreds. I've already lived through that enough in my life and I'm no longer interested in all that mess. Besides, I don't need a man to complicate my life. I have a routine, my snakes, and my books. That's all I need. *Mmm-hmm. If you say so.*

A few minutes later, I exit the forest and quickly cross the parking lot to my SUV. The eeriness of this place in the dark is starting to set in, and I'm getting legitimately spooked. Unlocking my SUV, I throw the door open and jump in, hitting the lock button as soon as the door closes. Then, I jam the key into the ignition and start the car.

As I throw it in reverse, I search my surroundings and my eyes latch onto the man standing at the opening of the forest trail. His head is tilted, almost creepily, and I can feel his eyes boring into me. My whole body tightens as it thinks about how he felt against me, inside me. Goosebumps scatter across my arms, pulling me out of my reverie. With a half-wave, I pull out of the spot and head out of the almost empty parking lot.

The State Park usually clears out by dusk, but it doesn't actually close until 10:00 pm; which worked perfectly for tonight's little meeting.

Another minute passes before I hit my first stop light, allowing me to find a song to play. I didn't want to sit in the creepy lot at night and search for a song. I've seen enough horror movies to know that's just dumb.

Pulling up my UnWind Playlist in YouTube Music, I click on shuffle and let the power of music do its thing. Boy Problems by Aston plays through the speakers in my car and my smile grows across my face. I reach over to the passenger seat, swipe the Medusa tee I stashed there earlier, and change out of my destroyed top.

Once the light turns green, I begin shouting the lyrics of the song into the air. I let it filter through my veins, allowing me to regain my balance. It should also help with the sub-drop that I'm sure I'll experience after today's scene. But, at least I got more than what I came for; a man ravaged me wholly and helped heal another piece of my broken psyche.

My therapist says it's normal for women who have been through trauma to act out their feelings. In some fucked up way, Primal Play and CNC help me regain control of my own body after so many others took it away from me.

However, my therapist definitely does not know about the other activities that I engage in. Regardless, I have found what works for me and I don't see any reason to change it now.

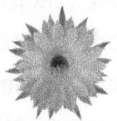

Just over an hour later, I pull into my gravel driveway. The drive from Huntsville filled me with peace and confidence. That man, currently known as "E," was hands down the best sex I think I've ever had. I always knew that "Good girl" was a thing for me, but that man played my body like it was his personal instrument. *Too bad I don't do seconds.* I may have told him differently, but that was just to appease him long enough that I could get out of there.

Clicking the button, I open the garage and glide right in; immediately closing it behind me and checking to ensure I wasn't followed. When the garage is almost completely closed, I shut off the car and flip the mirror down. There are leaves and dirt all up in my hair, reminding me of the fun I had tonight. Grabbing my brush from the glove compartment, I open my door and quickly remove as much debris as possible before brushing my hair into a messy bun. I giggle at the pun and roll my eyes at myself.

Once I'm done, I lean back in, throw my brush back into the glove box, and then grab my keys, phone, and wallet, which I stashed under the seat. Not ready to get cleaned up, just yet, I head over to the door on the far side of the three-car garage. Moving the black, steel shelving unit aside, I push on the wall until the familiar 'click' rings out. Releasing it, I wait as the small panel in the wall drops down, allowing me to enter my PIN. Once it turns green, I push the panel back, waiting to hear the locking mechanism click, and make sure it's flush with the wall. Not even two seconds later, the locks disengage, and a large door behind the hidden wall opens wide.

Stepping through, I turn and close the door behind me. I wait silently until the pin pad on the inside turns red, alerting me that I'm now safely locked in. Turning around, I head down the cement stairs into my basement. Well, basement-ish.

Recessed lights in the ceiling begin flicking on as they sense my movement; filling the space with just enough light that it doesn't blind me or the man sitting on the left side of the room.

His flabby, hairy self is still passed out in the metal chair I tied him to hours ago. *Rick Batesman* was a huge pain in the ass to get alone. But, as they all do, he underestimated me and I was able to drug him before he even had a chance to grunt a sound. Thankfully, we were right next to the van, so I just had to kick the sensor under the running board to get the door to slide open.

Dragging him down here was a problem since he's much larger than my usual targets. At 6 feet 3 inches and roughly 300 pounds of flab; yeah, it was hard. Thankfully, I prepared ahead of time, and he landed, ungracefully, into my van on a bunch of plastic wrap. I didn't bother to finish wrapping him until I got home since the sedative wouldn't wear off for hours, so I had plenty of time to slide his big butt in the van and get out of there before being spotted.

Getting him down to the basement was a whole other level of exhausting. I almost didn't make it to meet E. But, I somehow managed to wrap him up in the plastic I had, shove him out on the flat cart, and roll him to the door. The dirty jackhole slid all the way down the cement stairs; probably gaining a few new bruises and maybe a concussion. Then, I had to use the chains and pulley system I have rigged up to help get him in the chair. It took a lot longer than I wanted, but I still made it out in time to freshen up and then meet E. *And thank God I did!*

I lean against the light stone wall and take him in. Now that I've released my own demons in the forest, I can concentrate solely on this man's transgressions. His chest moves slowly and evenly as his head hangs forward. His blue basketball shorts hang off the chair, and his white tee clings to his sweaty, hairy body, staining it yellowish-brown. His black hair falls in front of his face, limp and lifeless. Kind of perfect, *considering...*

A loud snore rips through the room, causing me to jump. *Never have I ever...*

Rolling my eyes, I shake my head and approach the man who has more body hair than a Saint Bernard. It's quite gag-worthy if you ask me. *Nothing like the man I met tonight.*

Flashbacks of his hands on my body, his mouth in my most intimate places, and his dick... *Holy fork! That thing should be registered as a lethal weapon.*

I feel liquid heat pool in my panties, abruptly reminding me that I need to get cleaned up. But first, I need to deal with this stain on society.

Stepping towards my new friend, Rick, I slap his face a few times. The sedative I pushed into his system should be just about worn off, but he'll feel like a dirty butthole when he comes to; I should know.

"Ricky boy," I sing-song as I tap his cheek a couple of times. He mumbles incoherently then passes out again.

Annoyed, and more than ready for a bath, I walk around him and open the top left drawer of the giant Snap-On Toolbox parked against the wall. This thing is my baby. It's all white with blue handles. But the best part is that it has red LED lights underneath it. I only turn those on when I really have time to mess with these men.

Alas, that is not today.

I peruse some of my favorite knives before picking up my rainbow switchblade; the one without serrated edges. Nope, this baby is perfectly pointed and wickedly sharp. Flicking it open, I let the lights from above glint across the blade and admire the pretty colors.

A sound, somewhere between a snort and a snore, rings out again and pulls me from the peace this knife brings me. *Butthead.*

Rolling back my shoulders, I wander back over until I'm directly in front of him. Leaning down until my head is level with his, I take a deep breath. Then, I rear back and stab the knife right into his left thigh. The high-pitched wail that comes from his throat causes me to wince but I don't move.

His chest begins to rise and fall rapidly as his adrenaline kicks in. I wait, semi-patiently, as his brain begins making connections. I know the moment that he registers the knife in his thigh because his body immediately rears back, almost causing him to fall backward in the chair.

"Ah, ah, ah," I admonish playfully. His head snaps back towards me, and he finally realizes that I'm here.

At first, his eyes are glassy and confused. "Wh-what the. Where...Where am I? What did you do to me?" His confusion only lasts so long as rage begins to filter into his eyes and he spits out his final question.

"Oh, Ricky. You're in no position to ask any questions." I chastise him like a disappointed mother. His eyes flare and I straighten back up, towering over him. I can't keep the grin from taking over my face. I know men like him hate to be belittled or feel weak, so a female standing confidently over him is really going to set him off.

"Get me out of here, you bitch! If you really knew me you'd know I have people. People are going to look for me. And then you'll pay."

Clucking my tongue against my teeth, I tsk him again. Pulling my mouth down into a dramatic frown. "Oh! Say it ain't so." My exaggerated southern bell voice only pisses him off further. His face is puffy and red like a little angry bull.

Giggling, I lean down to look straight into his eyes again. "Too bad they'll never find you. Unlike the girls you raped, tortured, dismembered..." I trail off, lifting my brow high in challenge. And, like all the others, his face pales slightly before immediately running his mouth.

"I didn't do anything to those girls." He spits with a snarl. "I was already found innocent. This is bullshit." He starts fighting his bindings. Of course, I let him. I know for dang sure he's not getting out of my jacked-up, complicated ties.

After a few minutes of me watching him struggling in silence, he finally stops and sneers at me. But before he can spew any more crap my way, I reach over and yank the knife out of his thigh; twisting it just enough to make it rip open. Blood pours down the side of his leg and runs down the drain. His screams echo off the walls as tears slide down his face.

"Aw, what's the matter, Rick? Can't handle a little cut?" I bring the knife in the air and watch as his eyes widen in fear.

Pointing it at him, a sick sense of satisfaction washes over me as I watch him break. So, dang, easily. Just like I knew he would. Just like they all do.

With a scoff, I turn away and begin walking back to the stairs. I need him to feed into the idea that I may very well be leaving him, bleeding and pathetic and all alone.

I don't make it far before he cracks. "Wait!" He cries out.

I inhale deeply before pushing out the exhale, then slowly turn to face him. "P-p-please," he sobs as tears and snot roll down his face. "I'm so-sorry. I c-couldn't help it."

"You couldn't help it?" I growl. My eyes latch right onto his as I step closer to him, pointing the knife at him. My voice starts out low and menacing as I sneer, "You couldn't help but torture and rape them for days?" Step. "You couldn't help but dismember each of them while they were still alive?" Step. "You couldn't fucking help but scatter their remains in the ship channel?" Now, my voice is loud enough that it echoes around the room.

My chest heaves with adrenaline and pure rage. With one last step, the knife is pointed right at his big, fat nose. "You couldn't help it when you had your buddies at the station make the fingerprints and DNA samples disappear?"

"P-p-please..." He whimpers. The smell of urine fills the air, and I scrunch up my nose in disgust.

"You're pathetic." I spit out.

Standing straight, I wait quietly until he has the audacity to meet my stare; making sure I am the last thing he ever sees. "Rest in pieces, *Rick*," I grit through my teeth as I hold his shoulder with my left hand and stab him in the right side of his neck. Once the handle is flush with the skin, I twist and yank it out. Blood sprays all over my hand and the side of the room. I step back in time to watch as the light in his eyes vanishes and his head drops forward.

With a deep breath, I let the feeling wash over me. *One less vile piece of garbage walks this Earth.*

The sounds of the blood draining into the pipes underneath me signal that it's time to get cleaned up. Turning right, I go to the giant stainless steel sink and scrub my knife, hands, and arms with the antimicrobial soap I keep down here.

Once I'm satisfied, I stride over to the toolbox and gently place the knife back in its place, then slide the drawer closed.

Taking out my phone, I text my friend, Stu, letting him know I need a cleanup, but there's no rush.

With a final glance at *Rick*, I enter my PIN into the pad and pull the door open once it turns green. Stepping back into the garage and closing the door, I wait for the lock to re-engage before rolling the shelving unit back in front of the wall. Not that anyone can see it, but I like the extra layer of protection.

I meander across the garage and begin dreaming of a hot bath with lavender bubbles filling it to the brim. Unlocking the garage door, I go to slide off my slip-on Converse and pout when I see the red blood stains screwing up the pretty white laces and sides. "Durn it. Stupid Jerk," I mumble to myself as I kick off my shoes and rip off my socks.

Shaking my head, I walk into the mud room and throw them in the open washing machine to my right. With an aggrieved sigh, I slide off the rest of my clothes and stuff them in, as well.

Once I start the load, I walk through the kitchen and briskly make my way to my room. This girl needs a shower, a bubble bath, and a good book.

~CHAPTER 3~

Stu

My phone vibrates on my desk, temporarily distracting me from my computers. I've been holed up in my room for hours searching for the primary headquarters for The Crimson Knights. *Stupid fucking name.*

These assholes have been causing chaos all over the damn city and we really need to bring them down. So far, the only ones we've been able to catch are peons who don't know shit. And frankly, Even is about to go nuclear. I am so glad that he got out of the house tonight. I'm not sure where he ran off to, but hopefully, he comes back clearer. If not, I fear that Danny may curl into his darkness and not come out. He's so damn sensitive. Usually, Even is perfect with Danny, but he's been so terse lately that it's causing Danny to shut down in all the wrong ways. Add that to the fact that Charlie has been on a separate mission for two weeks... and, yeah, something has to give.

My phone vibrates with another message. I run my hand over my face and stretch my arms over my head, yawning heavily. Swiping the phone off my desk, I lean back in my office chair and glance at the screen. The notification banners show I have a message from Queen Bea and another from Even. My heart does a stupid little flip, and I click on Queen Bea first.

Queen Bea: Hey! Need a repairman. Same place, no rush. <kiss emoji>

My stomach tightens as my brain fantasizes what it would be like for her to actually kiss me. That woman has been the sole star of every one of my dreams for the last four years. But the security around her heart rivals that of the Vatican Secret Archives. I've never in my life been so thankful to stumble upon a crime in progress. I'm pretty sure that was the only reason she allowed me to help and, eventually, weasel my way into becoming her friend.

I've been sent to do recon on the Vipers' new leader. I'm not usually a face associated with The Vidar Mercenaries so I can snoop around a little. And, with my thin frame and multiple piercings, I blend right in with the rowdy crowd in this smoky bar.

I make my way through the bar with relaxed purpose and slide into a corner seat at the bar. This place is out in the middle of fucking nowhere but is known for its various MC connections. An older woman, maybe in her early fifties, slides in front of me behind the bar. Her hair is a whole rat's nest of brunette curls tossed into a messy bun on top of her head. And, no shit, there's a fucking raccoon on a leash, sitting on her shoulder like some kind of parrot. I've never thought about getting a raccoon as a pet, maybe I should.

"Can I getcha something, doll?" She drawls with a big smile. She reminds me of my mom and I can't help but smile in response to the graciousness that radiates off of her.

"'Rona. Dressed please," I respond, returning her smile. With a nod, she spins around and heads to the other side of the counter.

I've already clocked the Vipers, hanging on the other side of the bar playing Darts. They all seem relaxed and genuinely not looking to cause trouble but, I'll wait around for a while to see if I can pick up any conversations.

A beer slides in front of me and the older woman winks as she walks away, the raccoon's tail swishing across her back.

I chuff a laugh then dart my eyes around, taking in the other patrons hanging around. Clocking a few small groups of people, and a couple of loners at the bar, I free the lime from my beer, squeeze it in, and push the rind through the opening; allowing it to rest before taking a long pull. Just as I swallow down the glorious liquid, the front door opens and a trio of women walk in. They don't look like the typical country or biker babes but, in a place that is literally lined with antlers, I know this place always draws a curious crowd.

I'm just about to dismiss them before the two women in front part just enough for me to get a good look at the third woman. I almost choke on my beer when I see her. She's curvy in the most delicious ways. Her big tits look to be just over a handful and cause her navy Beautiful Badass shirt to stretch tightly across her chest but is loose around her stomach. She's wearing skinny black jeans with rips along the thighs and top of her shins and a pair of slip-on black Converse. Her dark brown hair has a scattering of blonde highlights and lies straight down past her shoulders. She's wearing just a little bit of makeup and, as she walks closer to the bar, I can see how the thin black eyeliner and mascara make her ocean-blue eyes pop.

Her head swivels constantly like she's expecting something bad to happen. She seems skittish, shy even, and definitely uncomfortable. The other two girls are happily chattering about something, but she keeps to herself; chewing on her plump bottom lip like it's a piece of gum. I want to take it in my mouth and suck on it.

As soon as I have that thought, the girls turn to her and ask what she wants. She orders a tequila sunrise; shocking the fuck out of me. She smiles brightly at the woman behind the bar and I have the overwhelming desire for her to smile at me like that. It completely transforms her face; like when the clouds part just enough that the sun peeks through.

Once the bartender slides their drinks over, the woman asks about the raccoon. I watch, entranced, as the bartender lets her pet the raccoon. She's so gentle and her eyes seem to shine with genuine interest and excitement. And, I won't lie, her round ass looks amazing in those jeans as she bends over the bartop to feed the raccoon a snack.

As the night wears on, I split my attention between The Vipers and the woman who continually pulls her shirt away from her stomach. It pisses me off that she's clearly self-conscious about it, and if I weren't here to do recon, I would absolutely try to get her number.

A new group of bikers enters the bar and judging by their patches; they are not part of The Vipers. Two things immediately catch my eye: 1) The Vipers abruptly stop what they're doing to look at the newcomers and 2) the woman I've been watching all night suddenly goes rigid. Both immediately set me on edge. I slide my phone out, keeping it on my thigh, out of sight, just in case I need to hit the emergency button I installed on our phones.

The newbies approach the bar and start ordering beer as The Vipers slowly make their way to the tables lining the walls. Even though the music is still going, the tension in the air thickens. The man closest to me is a little taller than me with a bald head and a long, scraggly beard. He's checking out the trio of women I've been watching and licks his lips like one of them looks particularly tasty. It's then that I realize that the woman I was eyeing has disappeared. The bathroom is on the far left side of the bar so it's very possible she slipped back there while I was sizing up these assholes.

Beers in hand, the newcomers stroll over to a pool table and begin horsing around. Baldie slaps one of them on his back and tilts his head towards the restrooms. The hairs on the back of my neck stand up as I scan the bar to double-check that my Beautiful Badass hasn't re-surfaced.

A minute passes, then another, and another. I throw down $20 and wander to the back where the bathrooms are. I don't want to startle her, so I check the men's room first. I could be completely over-reacting, which would be normal for my imagination. But something tingles in my gut, telling me that everything is not okay.

I check the men's restroom- Nothing. My heart rate picks up and beats loudly in my ears as I immediately turn back around and march into the women's bathroom. The empty women's bathroom. I quickly check the other stall and twirl around; my brows furrowed. What the hell?

Backtracking, I step into the hallway and notice a small door a few feet past the bathrooms. There are no lights back here so it's easy to miss. Without another thought, I march straight down the hall, slamming the door open.

The sound of the door clicking closed behind me is the only sound that breaks up the night-time symphony you can only get in the middle of nowhere. It's pitch-black outside. The only lights out here are around the front of the bar and don't illuminate much on my right before the dark woods swallow it up.

A sound similar to a grunt, and maybe a shuffle of gravel, causes me to whip my head to the left. As quietly as I can, I follow the wall of the bar until I hit the far corner, just before reaching the back. I take a deep breath, desperately hoping they aren't fucking like rabbits and my over-active imagination is making it out to be something worse. Slowly, I peer around the corner and see a big, dark mini-van. The side door is open; the dim interior lights are the only thing casting out the surrounding darkness. And... what the fuck?

I blink a few times, completely certain that I've lost my mind. But the longer I watch, the more I realize that I really am seeing this. Baldie is knocked smooth out and that little, shy woman I've been obsessing over is squatting next to the open door, trying to heave him into the backseat.

I stand there in complete shock for at least two minutes, watching her curse under her breath and struggle to get this man into the van. Eventually, curiosity wins out.

With a lazy grin, I shove my hands into the front of my black jeans and stroll over to the truck. "Need a hand?" *I ask playfully. She startles with a yelp, and I can tell her eyes have gone wide. Dropping Baldie's legs with a thunk, she quickly looks around to see if anyone else has caught her.*

"Um, he... he's. It's not what it looks like." *She stammers adorably.*

I suppress a smirk as I approach the van and really take her in. "It looks like you knocked out a man twice your size." *I purse my lips and tilt my head, trying to get a read on her.* "The question is: why?"

Narrowing my eyes I watch as a variety of emotions flit through the shadows of her eyes. But, the one I latch onto, is revenge. I feel my face drop and I swallow hard. Her lips tremble, and tears form in her eyes, but she straightens her shoulders, and I watch as she fills herself with confidence and bravery. Fuck, my dick is hard. She is a fucking vision.

"He deserved it. For what he did to me." *Nodding with understanding, I read the words she doesn't say. Whatever happened between her and this man was bad. And he either got away with it or threatened her not to talk. So, she took matters into her own hands.*

With a quick look around, I approach her and lift his legs. I nod in a silent command for her to hop in and grab his upper body so we can secure him and wrap this up before someone sees. She stands there for a solid twenty seconds, unblinking, mouth agape. "My Queen," *I purr sweetly,* "Kinda need your help here."

Her face scrunches up in confusion and it's so fucking adorable that I have to bite my lip to stave off a groan. I feel myself grinning the longer she looks at me. But, we really need to move. I tip my chin towards the van's interior, and she blinks a few times. Her eyes go wide, probably surprised that I'm offering to help instead of turning her in. Then, she scrambles into the back of the van to pull Baldie up by his shoulders.

By the end of the night, we had disposed of his body, and I learned through her raging at him, that he took what wasn't his to take.

Her body; and maybe a piece of her soul.

I held her after she broke down, drew her a bath, and even shared a little bit of what I do as a mercenary. I couldn't tell her the organization I work for, and still haven't, but she has allowed me to help her deal with her demons ever since. During the first year of our friendship, I learned that Baldie wasn't the first to take her body without permission; in fact, he was the *sixth*. Each one met their demise by my sweet Bea.

A little over a year ago, I finally tracked down the first offender; well, the first official one. I have a feeling she was used and abused a lot before that one. I made sure she was taken care of after she tortured him for 24 hours straight. He was the final person on her list, and I was both disgusted that ever happened to her and honored that she opened herself up to me and let me help.

Since then, she's been on a mission to take down any other assholes who have slipped through the cracks in the justice system. Thankfully, she finally let me take over the removal and disposal part after the first two years. It doesn't phase me after years of being with The Vidar Mercenaries, but it definitely made *her* spiral each time. Anything I can do to make her life easier, I'm all in.

My phone vibrates in my hand, bringing me out of my trip down memory lane. Looking down, I see that Even texted again.

> **E-Man:** Waiting on pizza rolls at DDs. Need anything before I head that way?

> **E-Man:** Also, I was thinking of going out tomorrow night. Maybe grab a few drinks at the bar around the corner that does karaoke?

My face turns into a scowl as I read and re-read his second message. *Hanging out at a bar with karaoke? Is he joking?* He barely tolerates Danny and me, and he's in a relationship with Danny.

> **Me:** Are you feeling ok? Fever? Hallucinations? How many fingers am I holding up? <middle finger emoji>

I huff out a laugh and flip over to Bea's message thread.

> **Me:** You got it, Queen Bea. I'll be there in about 30. Will let you know when it's done.

Even responds with a middle finger GIF, and Bea responds with a blue heart. My heart pinches, knowing the blue one means she's tumbling into Sad Town. I don't even think she realizes she does that. Her heart colors all give me a glimpse of her mood. *I can't have that now.*

I quickly type out a message to Even, letting him know I have to leave for a bit, but beers tomorrow sounds good. Then I grab my keys and head for Bea's.

~CHAPTER 4~

Even

I'm still reeling from my encounter with "B" today. Her big, blue eyes, the way her cheeks and chest pinkened so beautifully, and the way she squirted all over my cock. *Fuck, I'm getting hard again.*

Shifting my pants a little, I turn towards the counter as I wait for our pepperoni rolls. That woman has me fucked up ten ways to Sunday. I'd be lying if I said I wasn't disappointed she didn't want to talk outside of the app. For weeks, we've been chatting through the app. All of our kinks seem to line up beautifully and I know that Danny would love her. He's so damn shy, though. *Well, when it comes to women.*

We're both ready to have another woman between us, but he needs me to do the talking, the flirting, the wooing... he has no idea just how fucking amazing he is. He also falls hard and fast, so I need to make sure that whoever we bring in this time won't shatter his heart into a million pieces and cause him to revert back into his darkness.

"Even?" My name comes out as ee-ven, but I just smile and nod. I'm used to it by now. Not many people in the States use the spelling like we do in Norway so I'm always telling people that it's pronounced like Evan with an "a".

The guy behind the counter passes me our two huge boxes filled with cheesy goodness and I open them to make sure they include the ranch cups. With a nod, I throw five bucks in the tip jar and head back out of the restaurant.

This little shopping area is packed, but I quickly make my way through the vehicles in the parking lot, using the button on the remote to start it. It rumbles to life, causing me to smirk. It's not *super* loud, per se, but it does have a nice growl when it turns on.

Hopping up into the cab, I slide the boxes onto the passenger seat, then check my phone. I see Stu's last message and am relieved nothing else has come through. Our last mission was a total clusterfuck and we could all use a little break.

Closing out of the messages app, I start to search for YouTube Music. But, the app next to it catches my attention. Images of "B" throughout the night filter through my mind. Her fear was palpable but she was absolutely soaked by the time I caught up to her. The thrill of the chase is always intoxicating. She didn't give up easily, either. And I fucking loved it!

My cock stirs, yet again, as I think about how her pussy gripped me and milked me dry. My thumb hovers over the app as I consider sending her a message. Something in her calls out to me. I haven't felt like this after a hookup before; even when we first met Dana. But "B"... I have this urge to protect her, hold her, be her everything.

I swallow hard as I realize how utterly stupid that sounds. Yes, we've had some great conversations. She's sassy, she's intelligent, she makes up stupid words instead of cursing, and she cums so beautifully; even with leaves and sticks digging into her body. *Fuck it.*

I open the app and fire off a message, hoping I don't sound as desperate as I feel.

> **E:** Hey. Wanted to make sure you got home ok. Tonight was amazing and I really do want to see you again. Anyways, let me know when you're home. Or going to bed. Or whatever.

Closing out of the app, before I over-edit the message, I click over to my happy playlist and hit the shuffle button. The first chords of Dance, Dance by Fallout Boy ring through the cab of my truck, instantly putting a smile on my face. I don't know what it is, but I have a gut feeling that something good is headed our way.

When I get to the house, I click the button on the garage door opener and slide my truck right into the massive garage space. I immediately see that Stu has taken his truck for the night since his and Danny's bikes are still here.

With a shrug, I turn off the truck, hit the garage button, and grab the pizza boxes. I consider grabbing my tactile gear and bag but decide to wait until later. My little trip through the forest with a sexy woman has left me famished.

Once inside, I hang my keys up, set the boxes on the entry table, and quickly untie and slip off my boots. It's then that I notice how quiet it is. Eerily so.

Stu almost always has music playing and Danny uses TV, music, podcasts... anything to drown out the silence. He says that it's in the silence that the monsters in his head are the loudest. I know his childhood really fucked him up but we've worked really hard to try and prevent, or lessen, his triggers. And, silence is definitely one of them.

My steps quicken as the silence stretches out before me. "Danny!" I yell out, only partially nervous, for now. "I grabbed DD's!"

Veering off to the left, I slip into the kitchen just long enough to plop the boxes onto the island. I don't slow as I pass the island and head straight into the living room. With a quick scan, I see nothing is out of place; just the lone lamp in the corner by the entertainment center is on.

My feet move faster as I cross the living room and head down the dark hallway at the back of the house. I'm not sure what urges me to go this way, instead of upstairs to our room, but something is pulling me in this direction.

My heart races as flashbacks of Danny's last episode rip through my mind. *Blood, tears, pale... No. Just no.*

Once I hit the playroom door, I swing it open and immediately spot Danny. The regular white lights are on, but nothing seems out of place. Except for Danny; who's curled up on the California King four-poster bed. His breathing appears even but my eyes aggressively scan him as I rush forward. Reaching the end of the bed, I lean over and stick two fingers on his neck, desperately needing there to be a pulse. But, I don't even get time to check. Danny bolts up with a scream and clocks me right in the jaw. Pain splinters out from the point of contact, but I pay no attention to it. Danny's eyes are wild as he damn near falls backward off the other side.

Holding my hands up in a sign of surrender, I try to calm him, "Woah, there, Baby Boy. It's just me. I didn't mean to scare you."

He's panting and breathless, but eventually blinks a few times, allowing his gaze to focus on me. Once it does, he frowns in confusion before shaking his head quickly and reaching up to his ear. Pulling something out he gasps, "Fuck! You scared the shit out of me."

I grin at him and can't help but chuckle. "Sorry, Baby Boy. I just..." I trail off, feeling like an ass. Palming the back of my neck, I hear him chuff in surprise while looking at something in his hand. "I guess these little things do work. I fell right the hell to sleep. Hm."

My brows pinch with confusion as I try to see what's in his hand. Thankfully, he remembers I'm still in the room and slides across the silky sheets over to me. "I found an app that is supposed to help with sleep and it said it worked best with earbuds. I wanted to try it out while you were gone and, I mean, I guess it worked." He looks back at me with a shy smile and shrug of his shoulder.

Then, it's like a light bulb is clicked on: "Oh! How'd it go? I wanna hear everything!" He chatters excitedly. His brown curls flop around his head, and I can't help but laugh.

"Ok, Baby Boy. But, let's eat because I'm freaking starving!" He slides off the bed, palms the back of my neck, and pulls me in for a kiss. His scent envelopes me and the scratch of his blunt nails digging into my neck causes my jaw to tingle; and my dick.

Reluctantly, I break the kiss with a grunt and narrow my eyes at him. His mischievous grin brightens his maple-brown eyes, letting me know he is very aware of what he did.

"Let's eat!" He exclaims before bounding out of the playroom, leaving me to re-adjust the tent in my pants. *Oh, he's in so much trouble.*

~CHAPTER 5~

Beatrice

Tears form in my eyes, and I brush them away angrily. I hate crying. It's stupid and pointless and ugly. But, damn, this author is pulling at my heartstrings. The FMC in my book was kidnapped and is being tortured while her men- yes men; as in more than one- desperately try to find her before it's too late. This one is the second book in the series, and I already have a feeling it's going to leave me hanging by my fingernails.

I love these kinds of books: dark romances with multiple peens. It's easy to get lost in the characters and their trauma, knowing they will eventually be ok. It's *so* not the same in real life. Real life sucks you dry before you become worm food, vulture food, or shark bait. Regardless, it's stupid. There are no happy endings, just happy moments that fill in the gaps of deep pain. Ok, maybe not for everyone, but definitely for me. The only thing that makes me remotely happy anymore is ending perverted freaks before they have another chance to destroy someone else's life. Even sex is more therapy than joyful for me. Which reminds me...

E was, was... I don't even know how to describe it. I rarely have sex, and when I do, I make sure I'm 100% in control. Control has been repeatedly ripped away from me, and I refuse to let it happen again. Unfortunately, that means I have serious damage. But I found a way to cope. Even if I don't always orgasm, it's still so powerful to know that, for a brief moment in time, I made someone else feel good. It makes me feel not so...*disgusting, broken, ruined.*

But E was not only forking amazeballs, he actually got me to orgasm! More than once. I totally could have done without the embarrassing squirting incident. That's only happened one other time with the help of a little flower toy. I cried and threw the damn thing in the trash.

Images of E flit through my mind as I think of him all dressed up in the COD cosplay outfit. I'm glad he took the bulky helmet and headphones off after I started to run. That would have been such a pain to deal with.

But, when he caught up to me, he made the scene perfect in every way. I relished how he effortlessly moved me around like I'm not some size 18 woman. The way his pierced cock ripped straight into my soul was truly remarkable. My heart flutters as I think about his lips pressed against mine and feeling like our hearts were beating in sync. And, I can't help but remember the brief stab of guilt, remembering the way his eyes reflected genuine disappointment when I refused his offer to hang out. *Nope! Knock it off. It was dark. You didn't see disappointment. You saw the moon shining or something.*

With a heavy sigh, I place my book on the floor, just to the side of the tub so I don't get it wet. I'm clearly no longer in the headspace to read so I might as well just go to bed.

Sub-drop is apparently kicking in, and I'm in no mood to deal with it. But I refuse aftercare. It feels too intimate, and I no longer *do* intimate. The Dom who helped train me actually requested we stop seeing each other *because* I refused aftercare. He hated that I would end things quickly after a scene and then not reach out for several days to a week. I had explicitly told him I would be a good little subby, but nothing personal would be shared and, for me, aftercare feels *way* too personal. I can't allow my stupid, bleeding heart to catch feelings. Yes, yes... I know that's not really what aftercare is for, but I also know myself and refuse to be caught up like that again.

With a disappointed sigh, I lean forward, the bath water sloshing around me, and I unplug the drain. For just a moment, I get lost in the motion of the water swirling around before plummeting into the darkness below. And, before I can stop it, I'm transported to a different time.

Matt stands before me; his blonde hair seems darker since he just got out of the shower. I've been sitting on his bed for the last thirty minutes, finishing homework as I wait for him to take us to school.

Matt and I have been best friends for two years. We do everything together: movies, skating rink, parties, mudding...you get the idea. I even set him and his most recent girlfriend, Laura, up. Unfortunately, he also had me break up with her for him two weeks later. Boys. *He wouldn't even tell me why, but it doesn't really matter. He knows I'll always be on his side.*

Honestly, I've been in love with him since we met two years ago. I mean, he's a tennis player with pretty-defined abs and calves that look like they were perfectly sculpted. His deep hazel eyes are predominantly brown but in the right light, the green really shines through. At 16, he doesn't have any facial hair but that just means that I can admire the smooth curvature of his jaw. He's almost as drool-worthy as the guys in N'Sync. But, just like everyone else, he sees me as the "super sweet and funny friend." Insert eye roll here.

Ever since he broke up with Laura, though, I feel like he's been more touchy-feely than usual. Tugging on the hem of my shirt, brushing his hand down my arm after we hug; just little things like that.

Then, a week ago, he asked to pick me up from my bus stop every day so we could ride together. Of course, I jumped at the chance. That left us with plenty of time to hang out, have breakfast, and just joke around. I mean, Mom wouldn't really care. She's too busy yelling at my alcoholic stepfather. She will never know as long as we make it to school on time.

Today, he said he was running late, so we had to come back to his house so he could shower. I've been here quite a few times so I didn't mind. He told me his parents had already left for work so we won't have to worry about them fussing over us being late.

Which brings me to this moment—the moment that the Earth stopped turning—the moment that will forever be ingrained into my soul as a core memory.

Matt stands before me in nothing more than a deep blue towel wrapped snugly around his waist. A water drop leaves his hair, slides down his face, plops onto his chest, and continues its path down his smooth stomach. I swallow audibly before shaking my head and returning my stare back to my homework. I didn't mean to ogle him, but fork, he just walked out and stopped right in front of me.

An unfamiliar heat creeps up my neck and something in my core tingles. Am I getting sick?

I feel more than see Matt step closer to his bed where I'm lying and I have to consciously try to control my breathing. The lines on the page in front of me blur and my heart beats in my ears. Matt clears his throat and says my name. What's odd is it doesn't sound like his voice. It's almost deeper, yet so quiet I would have missed it had I been any further. "Bea?"

Confused by the question in his voice, I peer up at him and hum like I'm busy but still paying attention. Play it cool Bea!

Once my gaze meets his, my heart stutters. His eyes look darker, somehow, and his eyelids are lowered even though he's looking down at me. His pale cheeks are flushed bright red, and his chest shows a gentle panting rhythm.

"Bea?" His brow quirks up with the question, completely confusing me. I suppose he sees the confusion all over my face as he gently bends down and takes my textbook and notebook out of my hands, tossing them on the floor beside him. The move brings his face closer to mine, and I can see his pupils have grown larger.

Without my books in front of me, I feel exposed. We've been friends for so long, and the last thing he needs to know is how I feel. That would ruin everything.

"Bea?" He asks again, almost sounding amused, like he has a secret.

"Matt?" I tried to sound sarcastic, but I could still hear the quiver in my voice.

A smirk makes its way across his face, and his damn dimple pops out. Subconsciously, I lick my now very dry lips. The movement causes his gaze to latch onto my lips before he groans.

Now I'm super confused. "Matt, are you okay? What's wrong? Do you need to sit down?" I scramble to a sitting position with my legs on the side of the bed facing him.

He chuffs, shaking his head, and smiles wider. "I forget how innocent you are sometimes."

My brows furrow with confusion and the sudden change in topic. Before I can ask what the hell he's talking about, he leans even closer, putting his face right near mine.

"Tell me, Bea, have you ever touched a dick?" His warm breath ghosts across my face, and my eyes widen at his question. I mean, I mostly hang out with guys. My best friend is a guy. I'm not exactly prude but we don't talk about stuff like that.

"Wh-what?" I look away, embarrassment flooding my cheeks as I try to change the subject. Reaching down, I try to grab my book from the floor. "Stop jacking around. We're going to be la-."

And he drops his forking towel!

I lower my head and slam my eyes closed. I have no idea what to do. If I lean back up, I'll essentially be staring at his, um, thing. I can't do that. I'll just reach further away and grab my notebook while I'm down here. Yeah, that should work. Then he'll pick his towel back up.

Only, he doesn't. My heart stops beating when he moves over into my space. I can feel the warmth radiating off of his body as he towers over me. "Bea, come on. Just take a look then we can go. Unless... you're scared." His voice slides over my skin and makes me squirm. The challenge is clear in his voice.

But, then I remember: this is Matt. He loves to rile me up for no reason. "Whatever, Matt. Ha. Ha. You've had your fun; now get dressed so we can go already."

"Bea," I jump a little as his whispered word and warm breath fans across my ear, letting me know that he's leaned down right next to my head. "Trust me," he whispers as he glides his smooth hand down my arm. Goosebumps flicker across my arm and seem to migrate down to my nether regions.

I'm barely breathing, and I can't move, stuck halfway leaning over the bed trying to avoid his...member.

His hand trails back up my arm, then my neck, before stopping under my chin. "Bea. Look at me. Please?" The last word sounded much more playful, so maybe he's pranking me. Maybe he already has his briefs on. Little shit.

Keeping my eyes squeezed tightly, I let his hand move my face up to meet him. Once I'm sitting back up properly, I feel his thumb lightly *trace over my lip, before pulling it down just a little.* "Bea, If you can't look at my dick, how do you expect to look at a boyfriend's?"

The accusation makes me want to hit him and cry at the same time. He knows guys don't see me like that. Why would he say that?

"Ugh fine. I'll look at your thing. Happy?" *I say sarcastically and, frankly, a little annoyed.*

Opening my eyes, I take in his long, hard cock standing at attention. It bobs with each breath that Matt takes and there's a little, near-white bead of moisture leaking from the tip. It's forking long; freakishly so.

The heat in my cheeks spreads down my chest, and I stare up at him, thoroughly pissed off. "Happy, now?" *I spit.*

His smug-ass grin turns into something more mischievous, almost darker. His voice is low when he bends to whisper in my ear, "Not yet."

"Bea...Come on Beatrice." My brows furrow with confusion because I know that's not what Matt says, or does next.

Something warm and hard wraps around my front, and I immediately start fighting. I fight like I should have that day. I scream, and punch, and kick. A loud "Oomph" strikes through the fog of the memory but doesn't deter me.

"It's me, Bea. Come on beautiful, let me help you..." I scream out with a mixture of frustration and agony. My soul feels like it's being torn to shreds as the images from that morning flash through my mind.

Before I can convince my past self to do something different, anything different, something soft covers me. A weight presses down on one side as I'm laid gently on the other. Somewhere in my brain, I know this isn't the memory. *This didn't happen. I'm not there.*

So, I fight myself. I fight to break free of the memory and come back to reality.

A sweet, soothing voice shushes me and I can feel a hard body behind me. It's comforting, nice even, and... kinda sexy. *What the fork?*

That thought helps pull me back into the present. Blinking my eyes a few times, they finally clear enough that I can see my room. The fresh cream walls and various vinyl records displayed across from me instantly bring me relief.

I inhale deeply, hold for four, and then release. My face is wet and my eyes feel heavy and swollen. But, the soft palm that squeezes my shoulder paired with his raspy, "Good girl. You're ok," puts me in panic mode.

With a yelp, I shoot up from my sopping-wet bed and scramble to the edge, pulling the blanket with me. Turning quickly, I stare right into a pair of bright, blue eyes, and I immediately pray that the ground will open up and swallow me whole.

"S-Stu?" My voice is a panicked shriek as I try to scramble away from him.

As casual as always, he leans up on one elbow with that lazy grin of his. He appears to be fully clothed, so that's good, but his eyes are definitely giving away how much he's enjoying this.

"Easy, Bea. I hear the wheels turning from here." He raises his free hand in a placating gesture and his face softens. It's his calming face; one I've seen far too many times.

"What are you doing here?" I hate that my body trembles with shame, and I hate even more that my voice does, too.

Pushing himself up to sit, his back resting on the wall behind him, he explains, "You called for a repairman. But, when I got here, I wanted to see how you were doing. By the time I let myself into the kitchen, I heard you sobbing." He looks away from me, almost bashful, and shrugs a shoulder.

This time, when he speaks, it's even quieter; like he's sharing a secret he really doesn't want to. "I wanted to make sure you were ok. I knocked on the bathroom door and screamed for you but you wouldn't answer. I thought..." He trails off and runs his hand through his short pink hair, messing it up adorably. "I thought you were hurt and I wanted to help. By the time I unlocked the door, you were so out of it and your skin was turning blue. I just... I just wanted to help. So, I scooped you up and brought you to your bed to warm you up."

His voice is quieter, softer, and I now feel like a total jerk. "I'm sorry," I whisper and bat away the onslaught of tears that are still streaming freely down my face. "Just a bad memory. But, thank you for helping." I give him a shy smile and suddenly realize that I'm very naked under my weighted blanket. My eyes grow wide and my entire body flushes.

"Um, can I..." I peer down at the blanket partially covering me and hope he gets the hint.

It takes him a moment but when he figures it out, he barks out a laugh and shakes his head. "Of course, Bea, but...I've already seen it. You were naked in the tub, remember?" His brow quirks with his sexy grin and his eyes shine with amusement. I hate him. *No, you don't.*

My good friends, Shame and Embarrassment, bring a new set of tears to my eyes, and I look away from him. With a chuckle, he pops up on his knees, brings my head to his for a wet smack of his lips against my chubby cheek, and then hops off the bed. "I'll go make you some tea," He announces like this is an everyday occurrence.

"But, Beatrice..." I'm still recovering from the whiplash of his sudden playfulness so I barely notice his eyes raking up and down my blanket-covered body. Looking over at him, I watch his eyes meet mine and sparkle with something I haven't seen before. "Feel free to be naked around me all the time."

His cocky little smirk pops out a dimple, clueing me in that he's jacking with me. So, I do what any red-blooded woman would do, I take a pillow from behind me and chunk it at his head. The door slams shut just before making contact and I hear him cackle maniacally as he walks away. *Jerkface.*

Sliding off the bed, I quickly make my way over to my walk-in closet and find the closest pair of black leggings and a long, off-shoulder sweater. I need to make sure everything is covered. Stu may be the closest thing I have to a friend these days, but I still dress with as much covering as possible. Besides, my body always reacts to his presence and I've kept that junk firmly locked up. He doesn't need to know and I'm sure he has plenty of other people falling for his bad boy meets golden retriever vibe.

With one last look to make sure my belly and thighs are hidden, I glance back at my bed. Remembering the feeling of his body up against mine and his warm hands sliding down my arms causes me to shiver. I force out a heavy exhale and remind myself: *He's a friend. Nothing more, nothing less. Don't ruin this like you ruin everything else.*

Shaking my head, I rush to the bathroom to untangle my still-wet hair and brush my teeth. Feeling confident that the last of my armor has been snapped into place, I walk out of the bedroom and head towards the kitchen.

~CHAPTER 6~

Stu

I spent an hour with Beatrice last night. The entire time I made her CBD tea, I was willing my hard cock to stand down. He's been a moody bastard ever since we met her. Some days, it takes me forever to get myself off. Like he knows it's not her sweet pussy clenching around him. No matter. I'll gladly spend every day with my dick in my hand thinking of her while I bide my time.

When she walked into the kitchen, my dick tried to open my pants for me. The damn sweater may have hidden most of her body but it showed off her delicate collarbone and a little tattoo of three black birds. I wanted to trace them with my tongue and suck on her skin until a pretty bruise showed up.

Alas, I did not. I behaved like a good little boy. *For now.*

I know enough about her that I know she hates how she looks—not that she's ever said it out loud, but you can tell by how she dresses and carries herself. Eventually, though, I will worship every inch of her body until she knows just how gorgeous she is.

A message pings on my phone and brings me back to my current task. I've been running facial recognition for a few assholes who decided that using kids as drug runners was a good idea. Now, we get to end these dickheads for good. That's what we do, after all; Charlie is the leader and gets the information from our bosses; I find them, Even grab them and roughs them up a bit, and Danny, well, he makes sure the messages are received.

Speaking of messages...

Danny-Boy: Has E talked with you about last night?

I feel my brows frown in confusion. Last night I hung out with Bea for a little bit, even though she clearly didn't want to talk about whatever memory had her fucked up. Then, I let her get to bed while I finished cleaning up the douche of the night.

Once I got home, I heated up some of the leftover pizza rolls and drank a beer with the guys while we watched a documentary about a journalist who was killed because he got too close to revealing government secrets. Not that I was really paying attention, my mind was stuck on how Beatrice's warm, soft body felt up against mine. Even cold, wet, and terrified, she was intoxicating.

My phone buzzes in my hand again, oddly reminding me that I need to take my ADHD meds for the day.

Danny-Boy: I mean about the girl. The one he met on the app.

Me: Nope. Why?

Danny-Boy: He got this look in his eyes that told me he was feeling a lot more than usual. Not that I'm jealous, I just want to make sure, you know, she's vetted.

A smile forms on my face as I think about how twisted up these two already are. Danny is not jealous. Oh, no...he's intrigued, which, now that I realize that, could be more of a problem for him than Even. When Danny falls, he falls hard, almost to an obsessive point. Whatever Even told him about this girl, or maybe how he told him, has definitely sparked Danny's interest.

Me: Agreed. It's been a long time since anyone outside the four of us has been in our circle. And with the shit from the Crimson Knights getting worse, we absolutely need to make sure she isn't in danger; or dangerous.

Me: Send me what you have and I'll look into it.

Danny-Boy: (thumbs up emoji)

With a grin, I put my phone down and start clicking on various threads on the dark web. We've already been given another guy to look into who has connections with the Crimson

Knights, and I've also promised Bea I'd find her another friend to play with.

She looked tired-more so than usual after a cleaning- and I could tell the tears were never fully pushed back. Her whole aura was sad, almost depressive, and it felt like I was physically dying since I couldn't wrap her in my arms and help her carry some of those burdens.

I originally tried to talk her out of another target so soon, because of how last night ended, but she stood firm and shot me a hard look with those expressive blue eyes. And, yes, I'm a pathetic bastard because I just can't say "no" to her; but I can at least monitor her a little more closely. *At least, closer than the cameras I may or may not have situated in and around her house.* What? I need to ensure she's safe and I can't do that if I can't see her. At least, that's what I tell myself when I click over to the security tab and watch the cameras loop around her property. *Sigh.*

I have a bad feeling that she may be reaching her limit. But she was so adamant about needing another target that I quickly caved; I was afraid that if I didn't do it, she would go off on her own and get into trouble.

I know she doesn't have any family or friends who visit. She works from home, hangs out with her snakes, and binge-watches a random mixture of documentaries and TV crime dramas like *Lucifer and Castle.*

My unease forced me to slip a tracker onto her Suburban before I took care of the waste of space taking up her little dungeon. I already promised myself I wouldn't go full stalker and track her every second. But I mean, I am walking a fine line. Shit, all of the guys have caught me on multiple occasions checking her security feed. But, thankfully, they don't push.

They don't know who she is, just like I promised Bea, and only know that I help her sometimes. They also know she's not a threat to us *and* I have been harboring a crush on this woman for years. They've tried to set me up or go out and find some girl to satisfy my needs for the night, but, I can't. I won't.

Finding another candidate for Bea, I open our encrypted email chain and send her the details. Stanley Louis here sounds about as pompous as they come. He's currently inquiring about young kids. After a few more searches, I see that he likes to keep them for weeks at a time before dumping them back on their parents' doorsteps: broken, mutilated, and traumatized more than any child should be.

Anger courses through my veins as I think about this sick fuck who did something similar to me all those years ago. Not that I have to worry about him anymore. He's locked up tighter than Alcatraz after being caught red-handed. Literally. His wife came home early from some trip and saw him covered in blood with a little boy passed out on the couch.

Nausea causes me to sway and I realize that I am definitely still not over the fact that he's very much alive. If he ever had a chance to get out, I'd be the first one to greet him. Of course, he'd be dangling in our basement, but still, the possibilities…

A message on my phone brings me out of my all-too-frequent daydream. Seeing as it's almost seven in the evening, I lock my computer, swipe my phone, and head into the bathroom.

As I close the door, I check the message.

E-Man: On my way.

With nothing more than a thumbs-up emoji, I strip down and turn the shower on as hot as it will go. Another message pings, and I consider waiting but, I'm nosey and want to know what it is. Maybe it's Bea. My cock springs to life at the mere thought of her and I flick myself right on the tip. *Not that it matters, he likes a little pain with his pleasure.*

Opening the messages tab, I see that Danny has sent me the information for Even's little app friend. Thankfully, he also sent me Even's login, so I don't have to try to hack their system; yet.

A quick glance tells me a whole hell of a lot about her. She's clearly closed off. Her picture is of some kind of flower.

Curiosity reigns so I run back to my computer. I transfer the image into a search and see it's actually a flowering cactus called a Queen of the Night. It kind of reminds me of a little lion. The white petals in the middle form together like a small bowl and are surrounded by a flatter layer of petals. Apparently, the petals can also have varying degrees of pink and purple. It's pretty; unique. I like it.

Clicking on her profile, I see she's posted her height and made it abundantly clear she's not a petite thing. I guess she's had one too many run-ins with assholes who like her, but not her size. *Dumbass boys.*

What's even more telling is her list of rules. It basically boils down to, "Don't bother contacting me if you can't meet these rules." One includes no kissing and another requires that a mask be worn. *Interesting; but I'll file that away for later.*

The rest of her profile screams insecure and in control. All-in-all, she's not looking for something long-term. *Damn.* That could be a problem for E if he really is as wrapped up in her as Danny thinks. It's something to definitely bring up later. Thankfully, neither of them is talking about Charlie and me joining. We've done it in the past: shared women, worshiping them as they deserve. But, I haven't wanted to since I met Bea.

Not wanting to waste any more time, I link up the profile to my tracking system and let it run. If I'm lucky, I'll get some more information by the time we get home.

Jogging back to the bathroom, I'm suddenly hit with an idea. Instead of second-guessing myself, I type out a message to Beatrice and then pop in the shower. After last night, maybe it's time to push her a little. And maybe, just maybe, she'll let me in.

~CHAPTER 7~

Beatrice

My chonky Ball Python, Athena, slithers her way up my neck and into my hair, wrapping herself around her favorite yellow scrunchy. I never wear these thick things because my hair is so darn thin but Athena loves them. And, I love her.

It was love at first sight; or FaceBook post. One of the local businesses had her after being abandoned at the vet. She was only 6 months old and had to have surgery and a stupid amount of medications because of an infection due to stuck shed. She even lost one of her eyes. But once I saw the little lavender albino cinnamon roll, I knew she was mine.

Her pale yellow spots look perfect against her beige, almost lavender-looking, scales. She's perfect and so dang sweet.

My phone vibrates on the bed next to me as I finish my lesson plans for next week. Scooping it up, I click on the screen and see that Stu messaged me. It's not completely odd, but he already sent me my next target. And, as easy-going as he is, I have tried to keep that line drawn firmly in the sand that separates personal and professional. Although, he's the only one who knows about most of my tormentors. Well, he knows enough. Enough that when I asked him to track them down, he had zero qualms about me getting rid of the vermin from this world.

But, I could see it in his eyes. He knew. He always knew.

Then, last night happened. He's seen me lose control a few times but never, *never*, like that; fully immersed in a flashback. Unfortunately, he's seen me cry a few times. Heck, the night he caught me with Baldie and then helped me dispose of the body, he saw me cry in a blind rage. Then, he drew me a bubble bath and closed the door. He spent the next 15 minutes talking to me through the door while I relaxed into the heavenly smell of eucalyptus and citrus. From that night forward, he became my person. Well, as close to my person as I will allow. I still don't really talk to him about life or random things. We're not exactly the TikTok-sharing type.

But, last night was different. I was too vulnerable and, now, my feelings for him are getting harder to disguise.

Looking down at the message, I see that he's clearly lost his mind.

> **Stu:** Hey Queen Bea. Going out for a drink tonight and wondered if you wanted to stop by? It's a little karaoke bar not far from you. I'll even sing for you if you show.

What in the actual forkballs is going on? We don't do this. We don't hang out. We don't chit-chat. I mean, no more than surface-level crap; no matter how much he tries. And, I definitely do *not* go to bars anymore. Well, unless I'm tracking a target.

Hell, even the night Stu caught me a few years ago was a fluke. A few sort of friends from high school came home for a wedding or something and wanted to go to the cookey bar in the country. They had reached out to me since they thought it was more "my scene." Whatever that meant. But I ended up all too happy to see Baldie McButtFace walk in, so I suppose it wasn't a total waste of a night. Thankfully, I had a syringe in my purse in case of emergencies. And, the girls didn't give two craps that I left suddenly, faking a sickness. They had driven their own car, anyway.

Blinking back the memories of the past, I stare down at the phone and imagine Stu, relaxed at a bar, with no talks of demons amongst men. His piercings probably cause many people to flinch away but he's harmless. He has a bridge piercing, a loop through his right nostril, and a labret adorned with a single, silver hoop. Add in an eyebrow ring at the end of his right eyebrow and a circular barbell with cones on each ear and, yeah, he can be a lot to look at.

But, his smile, is *downright* panty-melting. It's like the entire universe could be distorted just because he smiles. And the dimples... *forks and spoons the dimples.* Swoon-worthy indeed.

More than that, though, he's always so playful and silly; even when I try my best not to crack, he can always make me smile. I also may or may not love that he doesn't stick to one hair color. When I first met him, his slightly shaggy hair was platinum blonde and messy in a totally laid-back, sexy way. He's also spectacularly rocked electric blue and pale purple. There was a, thankfully, short time that he had deep, dark black hair that made him look pale. Now, he's got a whole hot pink mop of hair. I won't tell him this, but he looks adorable with it.

The color may change frequently but he does keep the length pretty much the same. It's generally a tapered cut just above the neck and relatively messy all over. It's like he just can't be bothered with it. But no matter what he does, he still looks yummy.

Athena slithers down my neck and brings me out of my head. My cheeks hurt, and I realize it's because I'm smiling so hard thinking about this goofy man. *Nope.*

I chunk my phone on the bed behind me and slowly unwrap Athena from around my neck. I need to keep my head on, and no person, let alone a man, should have me smiling like that.

Just as Athena slides out of my hand and into her enclosure, I hear my phone vibrating on the bed. I stare across the room at it and hope to God it's not Stu. *He's probably just messing around, right?*

Ignoring it for now, I pad over to the bathroom and wash my hands with soap and water. Like any other animal, practicing good hygiene before and after handling is always important. Then, I turn off the lights and head out to the living room.

It's not much since it's just me. An oversized round swivel chair sits on the wall opposite of where my bedroom is. It's my favorite place to read or nap.

A 70-inch TV occupies most of the wall that separates my room from the living room. It's sitting on top of a long white-washed wooden entertainment center; complete, of course, with mini sliding barn doors.

A small white loveseat overlooks the massive backyard to my right near the windows, and a matching white couch is to the room's left. I cut tiny star shapes into my blackout curtains so that even when I don't want a lot of light, some still filters in— making me smile.

Crossing through the room, I pad to the kitchen and grab a Diet Coke, relishing in the *spshh* sound it makes when I pop the tab. Leaning against the white marble counter, I take a swig and find myself chewing on my lip.

Would it really hurt to have one drink? I mean, I could be there and back in time to finish the last few chapters of my book. And I don't keep alcohol here for fear I'd turn out like my ex stepdad: drunk and miserable with no life at all.

More irritated than I should be, I slam my soda down on the counter and stomp back to the bedroom to grab my phone. I can feel the anxiety in my body rising deep in my chest, and I can't tell if I'm going to scream, cry, or stop breathing altogether. *Easy, Bea. Breathe in for four, hold for four, breathe out for four...*

Opening my phone, I stare at Stu's message. My thumb hovers over the message bar, mocking me with emptiness. The words start to blur together as I zone out, thinking of all the reasons this is a horrible idea. Besides, he's probably just trying to be nice after saving me from myself again.

Finally, I reply.

Me: Thank you for asking. I know I was off yesterday, but I'm good now. Have fun.

With a partially contented sigh, I plop on my bed and notice there's a notification alert on the Kink-Finder app. Logging in, I open it and see that I have another match and he's already reached out.

Thoughts of E flow in and out of my mind. His hands on my body, the way every nerve-ending lit up for him. And that darn kiss. I'm pretty sure my soul left my body as his tongue tangoed so perfectly with mine. *Crap on a cracker. This is why I have a no-kissing rule.* My emotions are unreliable at best.

Clearing my thoughts, I check the message, which is a standard: "Hey. How are you?" Clicking on his profile, I start sussin' him out. I'm personally not worried about what he looks like, but I always store pics of the few I have met up with in my "If something happens to me" folder.

He's rather cute in a little brother type of way. But I don't even make it to his bio paragraph before declining. Once I see that he's 22 and a self-proclaimed "cougar hunter," yeah, no. That's not happening.

Clicking the no-match icon, I let the app do my dirty work. I may be strong in some aspects, but I know my heart is still a sappy mess that likes to spare others' feelings when possible. And, unfortunately, that has caused me a lot of emotional, physical, and sexual pain. *No, thank you.*

I've learned that the easiest way to prevent it is to avoid allowing anyone to get close enough to manipulate me. Which is how I've become a 32-year-old online teacher by day, a self-proclaimed vigilante by night, and the proud mother of four snakes. I have no family anymore and no friends, other than Stu and the men I bring to my war room.

The phone vibrates in my hand, causing me to yelp in surprise, and I laugh out loud because I am absolutely ridiculous.

Stu: Come on, my Queen. One drink. I'll pay!

Stu: And I'll sing to you. (smirk emoji)

I find myself chuckling at his antics and roll my eyes.

Me: It's not really my scene. But, thanks anyway.

Stu: Please! (pout emoji) One drink and I'll let you sashay that fine ass right out the door.

Rolling off the bed, I head towards the kitchen since I left my Diet Coke on the counter. I feel myself put a little extra sway in my hips as I figure out my response. I scoff at myself when I realize what I've done and fire back.

    Me: Whatever, Romeo. Use your charms on someone else and stop blowing smoke up my behind.

    Me: Also, thank you for another lead.

    Stu: Your ass is smokin all right. (wink)

    Stu: And, you're welcome. You can pay me for my services by coming out and having a drink with me.

Damn, this jerkface is really pushing it tonight. Usually, he lets me brush him off and move on. Maybe he really is worried about me. But, why? *We don't really know each other.*

    Stu: One drink. Promise. Cross my cock and hope to dive...

    Stu: Between the thighs of a beautiful woman.

My sudden burst of laughter actually surprises me. He's such a dolt. But, maybe he can be a friend. A real one. It's been like four years. And, one drink can't hurt. *Right?* I'll just make sure I buy my own, watch the bartender make it, and down it before anyone can mess with it.

Having made up my mind I quickly type out my acceptance before I change my mind. Then I head off to shower before trying to make myself presentable-ish. Just because I'd rather be in my night dresses and comfy shorts doesn't mean I should go in public with them.

Here's to hoping this isn't a terrible, terrible mistake.

~CHAPTER 8~

Even

Danny comes back with another round of beers and I tip my head in question towards Stu. Danny shrugs and shakes his head, signaling that he doesn't know what the hell is going on either. Stu is, well... he's Stu. He's always a little bouncy, a little loud, and a little goofy, but he has the heart of a saint and a brain that rivals Einstein when it comes to computers.

When our company first put us together 6 years ago, I was pretty sure I was going to end up strangling him. He has the attention span of a gnat and a body that moves more than a hummingbird's heart. But, after a few months of working with him, I learned to deal with it. Besides, he's loyal to a fault, smarter than anyone I've ever met, and he's been through his fair share of torture.

But tonight, my normally wired friend is off. Every time the front door opens, his whole body freezes and his eyes light up. Then, I watch as his shoulders deflate again and he goes back to bouncing his knee under the table.

"All right. Out with it." I grunt over the music. His head immediately snaps to mine and meets my hard glare. Whatever's going on, he needs to let it out.

"What?" he asks, looking completely confused. Tipping my beer bottle at him, I raise my brows and state, "You. What's wrong with you tonight? You're jumpier than usual. Are you OK?"

His heavy exhale looks almost painful as his eyes drop to the table. Danny's picking at his beer bottle label which means he's probably close to wanting to leave. This place is just starting to get crowded, and while he likes noise, he doesn't like being around a lot of people. It makes him incredibly uneasy.

Stu sucks his labret ring in his mouth and chews on his lip. When he releases it, he meets my eyes and a rare sign of pure vulnerability flashes in them. Leaning forward, I tilt my head and try to convey that we're here to listen; no judgment.

Taking a swig of his beer, he plops it on the table, then glances between Danny and me. "Ok. So, you know the girl I've been helping?"

I feel my brows pinch while one raises in confusion. "Queen Bee?" Danny asks.

Stu nods his head solemnly and seems to be figuring out how to say whatever it is that's on his mind.

"Ok. Ok. Here's the thing..." I can see he's really struggling because his arms are already starting to flail and he hasn't even started his little story.

And then, he releases it in one, full breath. "She had a bad night, and I helped calm her; which I've done before but not like this. She was, I don't know, Lost in her mind. Anyway, I wanted to make her feel better so I made her tea. Me. I did! I made her fucking tea and you know what happened next? We *talked*. Not about anything real or important, but it was so good, so perfect, so, damn, right. So, I may or may not have pushed her a little and convinced her to meet for a drink tonight."

With a deep, loud inhale, he sucks in a much-needed breath before deflating again. "I just, I'm nervous she won't come. But, I'm also nervous that she will." His voice was so low I barely heard it over the girl belting out her version of Olivia Rodrigo's *Bad Idea Right?*

I'm just about to tell him that he's a good man and to let what happens happen, but before I can formulate the words, in walks...B? *No fucking way.*

I blink my eyes a couple of times and squint, knowing for damn sure that won't help. She's here. Of all places in and around this town, she's right here! And, *fuck me*, she's beautiful. Her skin-tight, ripped black jeans hug every curve of her thighs and up her hips, disappearing underneath a long-sleeved, off-shoulder sweater with a picture of a skull with flowers growing out of its head. Her collarbone shows off that little tattoo perfectly and thoughts of me seeing it up close last night causes my dick to start knocking on my zipper.

Her hair is down, and her long bangs sweep across her forehead before being tucked just behind her ear. With the lights in the bar, you can't see the rose-gold overlay of her hair, so it just looks like a normal, blonde highlight. But, I know better. I've seen it, ran my fingers through it... *Oh shit.*

I almost groan with how hard my cock is but I don't want to startle Danny. He's already close to his limit. *But, what should I do? Do I tell her? Would that make it awkward?*

I mean, she made it clear she didn't want to meet outside of the app "activities," but she's right fucking here!

Then, those penetratingly gorgeous blue eyes find their way across the bar and she smiles; *fucking smiles!* Not the fake, half smile she awkwardly gave me either. It's real and bright and I feel drawn to her more than ever. Her smile actually moves her plump cheeks up and makes the heart-shape of her face look more pronounced.

I track her as she makes her way, almost shyly, through the bar; like it's not something she's used to doing. I notice her eyes flitting over every person and even see her darting glances at all exits. *Smart girl. Definitely been hurt before. Which makes sense, considering how she was last night.*

My heart beats like a bongo in my chest as she draws impossibly closer. Her smile dims only slightly but I can tell she has her sights set on someone near us. *Is it me? There's no way she recognizes me. I was in my full COD gear.*

Just as I think she's going to bypass us and head for the open area near the stage behind us, she leans in, just behind Stu. Her smile widens, and her whole face screams *flirty* as she whispers something to him, and I swear to God, my heart fucking stops. *What the actual fuck is going on?*

Stu whips his head and is almost nose-to-nose with how close she is and I can see his damn dimple pop out. His whole energy changes as he abruptly stands, hauls her up by the waist, and hugs the shit out of her, chanting, "You're here! You're here! You're actually here!"

For possibly the first time in my life, I'm stunned stupid. My brain ceases to function and nothing in this plane makes any sense. *Am I hallucinating? Dreaming? I mean, how the hell does Stu know B? And how do I get her to smile at me like that?*

She throws her head back and laughs as he twirls her around. After she slaps his back a few times, shrieking about being too heavy and to put her down, he slides her down his body. From here, I can see the light blush creeping on her cheeks and I find myself narrowing my eyes in annoyance.

He grips her chin lightly and leans down so they're at eye level. Just above the noise of the crowd, I hear him tell her, "Don't ever talk bad about this beautiful body again. You are not now, nor will you ever be, too heavy. Understood?"

I've never seen him take charge like that. It's a mind-fuck, to say the least.

Once he releases her, he flashes his broad smile, throws an arm across her shoulders, and turns to face us. "Beatrice, this crazy guy is Danny, and this Viking-looking mother fucker is Even."

Her shoulders hunch a little, and I see her brace herself in response. With a bashful smile, she reaches over and shakes Danny's hand. "Pleasure," she responds quietly, and time seems to slow as their gazes lock.

I glance over at Danny and immediately feel awful. Here I am having a mini-meltdown about a girl who has me twisted up and he appears to be two seconds from running across the country.

"Mine, too," he replies before immediately blurting out, "I mean, the pleasure is mine...too. Yeah." The contact is broken and she blinks like she was lost in her head or something. His cheeks flame with embarrassment so I subtly lay my hand on his thigh under the table, squeezing firmly to keep him grounded.

Beatrice's eyes dart down, and I see that moment she recognizes the act for what it is. I straighten my shoulders, not in the least bit ashamed of myself or Danny, but quickly realize I don't need to be defensive. Her gentle smile is soothing, accepting, as she reaches out her hand and shakes my free one. "Nice to meet you, too." Her voice is as sweet as I remember and flashbacks of her bound, gag, and at my mercy assault me.

"Pleasure's all mine, beautiful." My voice sounds a little huskier than intended, and I see Danny glance at me from the corner of my eye. Unfortunately, I'm a bad boyfriend because

I'm not concentrating on him. Nope, I'm watching that red heat wave I became familiar with last night stretch down her neck and spill out across her chest.

This night just got a whole lot more interesting. Whether that's a good thing or not is unknown. But, I'm absolutely interested in finding out.

~CHAPTER 9~

Beatrice

I knew this was a bad idea. Stu already had my body reacting inappropriately while he held my chin, and I just sat there like a good little subby. *Pfft. Moron.*

If my panties were damp before, they were soaked by the time I gazed into Danny's clear brown eyes. Not only were they uniquely transparent-looking, but I felt like his soul called out to mine. Like I could jump inside of his eyes and we could float off together. *Stupid right? Yeah, I know. And this is why I don't leave the house.*

To top it all off, there's a Nordic God at the table. I'm pretty sure his deep voice caused my panties to incinerate on the spot. *Meh, one last thing to have to wash.*

Stu grabs me by the hand and promptly rushes us over to the bar. He's so adorable yet, strangely, edgy. It's such an odd mixture but it works for him. His hair is playfully messy and his biceps twitch as he leans on the bar top to flag down a bartender. His navy blue shirt fits snug across his arms and chest.

He's not huge, like Even, but he's built, strong and fucking tall. I'm a whopping 5 foot 4 inches so he must be at least 6 foot 3.

As the bartender takes our orders, he leans over the counter and pulls a few napkins out of the pile, allowing me the perfect view of his back muscles flexing through his shirt and that rear. Holy guacamole. His rear is perfect. Delicious even. *And off-limits. What the hell is wrong with you?!*

Just as I chastise myself, he returns that sexy smile back to me. "I can't believe you're here! I'm so excited. Oo! Oo! What song do you want me to sing you?" He's jumping up and down like a kid who was just told he's going to DisneyWorld. His excitement is infectious, and I find myself laughing along with him, struggling to keep my voice firm. "No! No songs. One drink. Besides, you can't leave me with guys I don't know. That's just awkward." I pointedly grimace and shake my head.

"Nah, they're good guys. We work together. Well, we live together, too. But, yeah. We're a team through and through. Best guys I've ever met. And I trust them with your life, which is *not* something I do carelessly."

I'm not sure why, but his words—and maybe the passion in his tone—cause me to relax a little. I nod and smile, but I can't respond as his blue eyes zero in on mine.

For just a moment, it feels like everything stands still. His smile is so broad and the lights in the bar cause his bright blue eyes to look almost cerulean. Subconsciously, I find myself licking my lips and chewing on the bottom one. His eyes dilate as they catch the movement and only meet mine again when I release my lip from my teeth.

"Stu..." My whispered question is cut-off by the bartender clunking our drinks onto the counter.

"I put it on your tab, sweetie." She says with a little twang. I'm secretly grateful for the interrupting bartender because I'm fairly certain I was about to make a fool out of myself.

"Thanks, Linda!" He shouts out as she makes her way down to the other end of the bar. He scoops up both drinks in one hand. With a nod of his head, he grabs my hand and pulls me back towards the table. I realize he's done that twice now, and I haven't recoiled or tried to remove his hand. It's *nice*, actually. Warm and firm against my palm. His hands are soft, but he's a computer guy, so I guess that makes sense.

Thankfully, we get to the table before I can overthink it. However, it doesn't escape my attention that he oh-so-subtly shifts his chair closer to mine once I get settled. *Oh boy. It's just one night. He's trying to make me feel comfortable. It's nothing. It's fine.*

And that's the mantra I repeat in my head for the next thirty minutes as his hand, knee, or thigh constantly brushes up against me.

Fork nuggets. This is bad.

~CHAPTER 10~

Stu

I still can't believe Bea is here. She never goes anywhere; she even gets her groceries delivered. But here she is, in all of her beauty. I thought for sure I was having a stroke when I heard her sweet voice whispering in my ear about buying her a drink. Once I turned to see her, though, I skipped the stroke and went straight for heart failure. Her eyes were sparkling with amusement, and she was so damn close I could smell the Champagne Toast body spray she uses.

Even's been unusually quiet tonight, almost contemplative. Danny, on the other hand, is fully out of the shell he's been hiding in. Unsurprisingly, Bea has totally fallen for his crazy-boy charm. When he's high, he's the most charming man you've ever met; could probably charm the pants off a nun. But when he's low, shit goes one of two ways: either people die, or we have to watch to make sure *he* doesn't. Either way, Even and I much prefer this side of Danny; the one currently rambling about the differences between the Dumbo Octopus and the Coconut Octopus.

I regard her as she leans in and eats up every word, giggling as he flails his arms around, imitating how the Coconut Octopus can "walk" on two limbs like a human. Her smile lights up the entire room, and something deep in my soul calls out to her, praying for a chance to see it every day.

Danny suddenly trips over the chair next to him and damn near crashes to the floor. His carefree laughter rings out and causes a chain reaction. Even, Bea, and I quickly follow, laughing until my side hurts. And just when I thought I couldn't fall any harder for this damn woman, she snorts. Yes, snorts. One second, she's laughing, then she tries to inhale, and the cutest pig-like sound comes out. I swear to all things unholy that it was the most adorable thing I've ever heard.

Of course, embarrassment takes over; her eyes go wide, and she slaps her hand over her mouth. I give her a lop-sided smile and lean in before whispering, "That was the cutest thing I've ever heard, and I will try to hear it from that pretty mouth every day."

Her forehead unwrinkles, but her eyes stay wide as she takes in my words. The other two have also stopped laughing, so I know they're watching as she battles something within her mind.

I'm just opening my mouth to assure her it was cute, and in no way were we laughing at her, when she quickly stands up, almost knocking her chair over. "I've gotta go to the bathroom!" she exclaims, then slips through the tables leading to the back of the bar before I can even blink.

I watch her ass sashay in her jeans until she disappears around the corner. I can feel myself smiling like a buffoon, but I could care less. This is quickly shaping up to be the best night of my life.

The moment Beatrice slips out of view, Even groans, rubbing his hands roughly across his head. Danny slides back in his stool, still laughing at his own goofiness. "What's up, man?" I call out across the table.

"So, that's her? That's the woman you've been falling all over for the last four years?" His voice hitches a little. For the first time all night, I really look at him. He looks distressed; not his clothes, but his face, his eyes.

Tilting my head, I wait until he meets my gaze, flicking briefly over to Danny, who also looks bewildered by our dear friend's suddenly troubled state.

Staring back at Even, his words finally settle into my mind. *Shit, he doesn't approve. Or maybe he knows she's way out of my league...*

Clearing my throat, I take a swig of my beer and look anywhere except at him. They know enough about Bea to know I obviously care for her, but I'm absolutely not ready for them to start analyzing how deep those feelings go. Especially if they don't approve of her for some fucked up reason. And, if anyone can see through me, it's these two.

"Uh, not falling over. Just..." I shrug a shoulder as I use a napkin to wipe away an invisible stain on the table. "We're friends."

"Bullshit!" Danny exclaims with a laugh. "We've only been talking to her for thirty minutes, and I can totally see the appeal. She's sexy, curvy as fuck, and her smile..." He fists his hand and bites the knuckles while he groans and flutters his eyes like he's having an orgasm. *Fucker.*

Shaking my head and rolling my eyes, I shove him a little while chuckling. "Fuck off, D." He bats his lashes at me, then leans in, snuggling onto my shoulder and wiping away a non-existent tear. "Aw, Love, our little boy is in love." With a dramatic sniffle, he pulls away and slams his lips onto Even's.

My brows raise to my hairline. Danny's not one for PDA, but he's obviously just as affected by Bea as I am. Danny groans and then releases Even, who looks as stunned as I am. Then, as if nothing happened, Danny leans back in his chair and gulps the rest of his beer down. Even's dazed expression causes me to chuff a laugh, and I have to say, I love seeing a dumb-founded Even.

Eventually, he blinks a few times before clearing his throat. Then, he leans forward and looks me dead in the eye. "No, seriously, I have to tell you—"

Bea walks up and stands almost awkwardly next to me, demurely moving her hair away from her face and maneuvering it behind her ear. The pink snake shaped like a heart attached to her industrial barbell catches my eye before I look back at her and smile.

"So, um," she trails off momentarily, chewing on her pouty lower lip. My cock presses against my jeans, and I subtly move my lap away from her, just in case. "I should, um, get going. But, thank you, Stu. I really needed this tonight."

She places her hand on my forearm, and her eyes sparkle with pure vulnerability. For a brief moment, I consider kissing her. I've thought about it for years, but never, not once, has it felt like she was open to it—open to me.

But, all too quickly, the moment slips by as she smiles again, squeezes my arm and turns towards the other two. "Even, Danny, it was truly a pleasure to meet you both. Maybe I'll see you around." She says with a timid smile before flouncing out of the bar before any of us has a second to respond.

Like an idiot, I stare at the now-closed door as if she may magically come back. But, as usual, she's here one second and gone the next.

A triple beep on my phone arouses me from my stupor, and I pull it from my pocket. Knowing the triple beep is tied to my search program, I immediately open the app that connects to my home computer.

"Hey, Danny, I just got the information you were looking for," I say casually.

But, once I click on the results page, I freeze. My mind can't connect the information in a logical sequence. It doesn't make sense.

I stare at the information for longer than necessary, desperately trying to figure out if I somehow mixed up the tracker codes. I know I didn't. I wouldn't.

"Bea's the girl!?" I say incredulously as I whip my head across the table to Even. The moment our eyes connect, I see it-the truth.

And now things are much more complicated than ever before.

~CHAPTER 11~

Beatrice

W*hat in the forking crapballs was I thinking?* I mentally chastise myself as I all but sprint through the parking lot. My SUV comes into view, and I feel half the weight of my terrible decisions lift off of me.

I got comfortable. *Too* comfortable. Between Stu and the ridiculous attraction I've felt towards him for years, Even lookin' like a gosh-darned lumbersnack, and adorable Danny with the darkness that calls out to mine, I'm overwhelmed, embarrassingly soaked, and downright needy.

Unlocking the car, I dive in, close the door, and immediately lock it again. Pulling out, I carefully make my way through the lot, then pull up at the stop sign at the exit. A quick look tells me I'm alone, and no one else is waiting to pull out.

"Uuugghhh!" I growl out and pound my palms against the worn steering wheel. "Stupid fracking idiota!" I shake my head, more than a little annoyed at myself, before slipping my phone out of my pocket and pulling up the music app. With a quick glance around, I click on my Pent-up playlist and press play. I

Stand Alone by Godsmack beats through the speakers, and I lose myself to my frustration, simultaneously reminding myself that I'm a fierce, independent woman and I don't need anyone.

The drive home helps clear my mind as much as possible. But there's still a buzzing, a tingling tangling deep under my skin causing me to feel unsettled.

Pulling into the garage, I check my mirrors as the door closes behind me before killing the engine. With a heavy sigh, I drop my head to the steering wheel; palms squeezing almost painfully across the leather.

I don't even know what I want but tonight was definitely a reminder of why friendships don't work. I mean, I'm obviously damaged. I was panting like a dog in heat over three men tonight. And one was the only friend I have. *What the schnitzel is wrong with me?*

My phone vibrates with a notification and I groan out, assuming it's Stu checking on me. I'm not mad at him. I hope he knows that. I just... I had to get out of there.

Leaning up in the seat, I swipe my screen open and see that it's a notification from a video app I use. My whole body immediately reacts; goosebumps prick my skin, my core throbs in response, and I can feel my body temperature rising. *See, damaged. Yet another guy I'm lusting over...*

Curiosity and a bone-deep need to help shake off these stupid feelings has me clicking on the app and opening up the messages.

Alpha: Finished my last job and all I want to do is see your pretty pink pussy clamping down on a vibrator.

This man has never minced words and, crap, it totally works for him.

I debate for a moment, like maybe a whole second, before responding.

> **Omega:** Just got home from a night out. When do you want to meet?

The green dot shows me he is currently on so I know I won't have to wait long for a response.

> **Alpha:** Five minutes?

> **Omega:** Yes, Sir.

> **Alpha:** Good girl.

> **Alpha:** Lacy pink panties, the ones with the open crotch so I can see your dripping cunt.

I press my thighs together, already squirming for his direction.

> **Alpha:** The little pink mask that leaves your mouth exposed and the white button-up you bought.

I grin because I bought that shirt for him. He always starts our videos with a button-up and I wanted to play into the fantasy of wearing it after we finished. But, since we don't actually meet, I bought one.

Omega: Yes, sir.

With a deep breath I climb out of my car, pocketing my phone, and race into the house.

In less than three minutes, my hair is re-fluffed, as much as thin hair can be, and I'm wearing the too-large white shirt, completely unbuttoned. My boobs are large enough that it prevents the shirt from opening fully; not that it will stay that way. The shirt is so long that it takes me almost a full minute to roll the sleeves up past the elbows. It hangs just below my butt and makes me feel all kinds of sexy.

Slipping into the crotch-less panties, I grab my laptop and shake the mouse to life. Navigating to the streaming system, I log in, then run back to my closet to throw on my mask.

Just as I sit back in front of the computer, his video feed goes live.

"Oh baby how I missed you." His growly voice sounds tired and I have to force myself not to ask what's wrong. No personal stuff. Ever.

"I missed you, too," I all but whispered, secretly embarrassed by the truth behind the pleasantry.

His face is masked in dark shadows, only granting me the extreme privilege of taking in his bare chest and arms. His wide chest is lightly dusted with light brown hair across his pecks before a thin line trails alllll the way down, disappearing into his open jeans.

With a smirk, I sass, "I see you've already started without me. Or you finished with someone else..." That thought shoots a strange pang of jealousy through me and I have to catch my face from showing my confusion.

"Yes, baby. As soon as I stepped out of the shower, I messaged you. Didn't bother zipping the pants when my dick was already hard thinking about you."

I feel the familiar flame of lust brush across my cheeks and I duck my head.

Clearing his throat, he chuckles before abruptly changing the subject. "I see you added another vinyl to your wall." He comments with a nudge of his chin.

Looking behind me, I locate the newest album on my far bedroom wall. Turning back, I feel a smile pull across my lips as I divulge, "Yeah. I found it at a garage sale. I have a real one that I play frequently on my turntable but this one was perfect for my wall. It was all scratched and stuff, but Prince is one of my top 5 favorites of all time."

"And let me guess, Purple Rain is on your top-songs list." His tone is playful, and not the least bit condescending, so I answer truthfully. "More than you know."

Silence descends over us, making me squirm. *Shoot. That was too personal. Time to get this back on track.*

With a naughty little grin, I lean back so he has a full view of my bare chest, my boobs barely hanging onto the sides of the shirt. I gently trail my fingers over my collarbone and down the valley between them before circling my right nipple through the fabric.

"How much did you miss me?" I purr with all the false bravado I could muster. A sex kitten, I am not.

His answering groan makes me smile and I roll my chair back a little further. "Did I say you could move?" His low voice sends a thrill down my spine.

"No sir," I answer coyly. "But how will you see how wet you make me if I don't move back?" I know I'm riling him up, but he loves it; and so do I.

With another low growl, my body lights up. I feel the flush expanding down my throat and splotching across my chest. I whimper in response.

He suddenly stands up, shucks his pants, and frees his glorious cock from the confines of his briefs. I briefly say a prayer for any woman he has actually had sex with because, dang! The man is thick. It's not super long, maybe 5-6 inches, but I bet even I would have a hard time putting my mouth around him. Add the looped Prince Albert piercing and the looped Lorum, yeah, that poor girl would be walking funny for a week.

"Do you wish I was there, baby? You're licking those sexy lips like you want a taste."

I jolt, slightly embarrassed I had been doing that. "Y-yes," I whimper as my pussy clenches around nothing. Because, yes, I would happily suffocate with that man's perfectly colored, perfectly shaped penis down my throat. And that's a hill I'd gladly die on.

He sits in his chair and leans back, allowing me to take in this beautiful specimen fully. I swear he must be a quarterback. You don't get shoulders and arms like that without putting some serious time in the gym.

Wrapping his giant hand around his cock, he tugs roughly, just once, and I watch as his abs ripple with pleasure.

"Ok baby, I've made you wait long enough. Lean back for me and spread those creamy thighs."

I almost choke on my tongue. This is not the first time we've done this but I swear it annihilates me every time.

"Yes sir," I moan as I push my chair back enough that I can spread my legs wide for the camera.

He groans low and long, stroking himself slowly but I can see his fist tightening with each pass.

"Slide your hands down your body, baby. Imagine they're mine and I want to explore every inch, every curve, and hear every whimper."

My body is already shaking with desire as I begin to explore. "Move the shirt off those perfect breasts," He pants; clearly worked up as much as I.

I delicately run my fingers across my chest and nudge the fabric aside with just enough force that it moves off and away from my body. I know he can't see much of my belly because I've semi-wrapped the shirt around it.

As I repeat the movement with the other side, my nipples peak with the cooler air. I hear his panting getting deeper and more unstable.

"Good girl." A bolt of arousal shoots all the way through my toes and I moan out.

I almost don't hear his next command but his voice is so dark and dirty that it penetrates the fog. "Play with one breast while you show me how wet you are."

I take a peek at him and see that he appears to be physically restraining himself from jerking off. The head of his cock looks angry and dang near purple as he squeezes the base.

I focus on his body, how his muscles contract with each breath, and slide my fingers under my hood and between my folds. A pained grunt leaves him, causing me to grin as I pinch and tug on one nipple while scooping up my juices with my other hand. *Crackerballs. I'm soaked.*

The feeling of having him watch me, desire me, while I drag my fingers through my arousal overwhelms me and I throw my head back and groan. My right hand continues to pluck and pull my nipple- not that it does much for me- and my left hand continues to slide around until I come up and press on my clit. My back bows as I moan out and I can hear Alpha suck in a deep breath.

"Show me, baby. Right now." His low voice quivers, telling me that he's as keyed up as I am.

Blinking my eyes back open, I trail my soaking fingers from my core, up my body, and straight to my mouth. Then, I bury them deep in my mouth like I would his thick cock, swirling my tongue around my fingers until they are cleaned.

His low groan and flexing of his arm catches my attention, and I'm memorized; intently watching as he slides his hand up and down his thick cock.

"Good girl. Now, put your fingers deep inside that needy little pussy. I know it needs to be filled up. Since my cock isn't there, you'll have to do it for me."

I groan around my fingers before letting them go with a *pop*. He moans low and long, his sexy freaking forearm giving me enough rub club material to last a year. *I wanna trail every vein...*

"And, I'd let you. Now, stick those fingers in your pussy before I go dark." Oops, apparently I said that out loud. *Wait...*

The jerk is chuckling deep in his chest, clearly remembering the last time he did that. He turned the camera off but left the mic on. It was the sweetest damn torture. But, not today. I can't today. I *need* this today.

I obey immediately, plunging two of my fingers deep inside. I cry out as I feel myself clenching around my fingers and arousal drips down my hand.

A devious chuckle vibrates through the speakers and I have just enough brain power to continue pumping my fingers as I open my eyes and watch the screen. "Good girl. I'm glad you learned your lesson last time. Now, fuck yourself on your fingers and play with your clit. Show me how you get off."

A rebuttal sits on the tip of my tongue but I let it go. He doesn't need to know I don't have a "thing" that gets me off. Sometimes, I can; most times, I can't. Plastering on my best fake smile, I prepare for the inevitable and play my part. "Oh, God! Yes, sir."

I go to town on myself. Pulling every move, every trick, every flick of the wrist I can think of. The room is filled with nothing other than our moans, groans, and heaving breaths. "That's it, baby, fuck that pussy. Fuck it like you would my cock."

I groan as I clench again, causing my movements to stutter. "Good girl. Now rub that little clitty for me."

His breathing has picked up, and I open my eyes long enough to see that his gorgeous abs are beginning to shine with sweat.

Pretty soon, we're both worked up, panting, sweaty messes. But, I just can't quite get to the line. Thankfully, he calls it. "Cum for me baby. Come all over your hand."

I screw my eyes shut and lean my head towards the ceiling. My hand stills deep inside me and I scream out, "Alpha!!!!" The tell-tale sounds of him finishing hit my ears, and I add a few little body jolts for good measure.

I am well and truly spent. No, I didn't have an orgasm, but that doesn't mean it didn't feel good. This was exactly what I needed.

A lazy grin forms on my face as exhaustion begins to close in. Alpha is wiping his sticky cum off of his abs, heaving from the exertion.

"Omega, that was..."

I smile warmly at him, dropping my feet to the floor with a thud, and straightening as much as possible in my chair. "Yeah, it was."

Tucking the sides of the shirt back around my breasts, I officially feel closed off again.

"Thank you. It was good to see you." I can see him nodding a few times and wonder if he heard me. Just as I'm about to repeat myself, he blurts, "Maybe we can hang out next week. Coffee? Dinner? Something?"

My entire body freezes and I stare at the screen. *Why are all the men in my life suddenly wanting to hang out? Is this a prank?? Every one of them knows the score. Maybe I'm sleeping. Or, I need sleep and I'm delirious.*

Yeah, that checks out.

With a forced giggle I wave my hand out. "You're so silly, Alpha. That's not in the rules and you know it." I force a laugh.

He looks like he's about to say something but my phone vibrates next to me. *Saved!*

I pretend to look over and grimace. "I'm sorry, I've got to take this. Thank you, again, Alpha. We'll do this again soon." I end the rushed goodbye with a smile and a wink before exiting the browser.

With an exhausted sigh, I slump in my chair and fling the mask from my face. It's then that I realize I didn't cover the tattoo on my right arm—the big geometric one with a Stargazer Lilly on it. Ah, *cracker*.

This is why I don't do last minute meetings.

I roll my eyes and lift out of the seat. There's nothing I can do about it now. Hopefully, he was too wrapped up in getting off to notice.

Swiping my phone, I open it and walk towards the bathroom so I can hop in the shower and clean off this strange night.

I see Stu left me a message, but honestly, I'm not ready to talk to him yet. Something shifted today, and I'm not afraid to say that I'm too big of a coward to face it.

I'm also much too exhausted to analyze it—for now, anyway.

~CHAPTER 12~

Even

One Week Later

I growl in frustration as I snap the boxing gloves off my hands. Throwing them onto the mat, I stomp towards the counter on the other side of our gym and angrily swipe my water bottle, guzzling half of it before taking a breath. I spent thirty minutes running my frustration out on the treadmill before trying to take it out on the heavy bags. And yet, here I am, still reeling from that night.

When Bea walked up to Stu last week, I swore I was seeing things. We met at the forest an hour away, and yet, she was close enough to come to the bar near our place. And she's friends with fucking Stu! *What the hell?*

He rarely talked about her but the little bit he did say... he left out details. A lot of details. All those curvy, luscious, sensual details. *And now my cock is searching for her again. Fuck.*

Scrubbing a hand roughly through my hair, I yank the ponytail holder out and head out of the gym. Stu tried so hard to hide his disappointment, even heartbreak, over Bea being the woman I met with the other night. We both know *I* didn't know; I never would have hurt him on purpose. But the look he gave me before abruptly standing and walking out of the bar last week almost broke me. He's my best fucking friend, one of three people I trust more than myself in this world, and he's hurt. Badly. He's been actively avoiding me all week. Only reaching out by text, and only if it's business related. He won't even open his bedroom door; he just cranks up the music and drowns me out. I've had to resort to Danny bringing food to him just to make sure he's eating.

Opening my door, I realize that I don't even remember stomping through the living room or coming up the stairs. My thoughts are all tied-up and tangled in Bea and Stu and... *fuck!*

Stripping out of my clothes, I toss them into the hamper before walking into our massive ensuite. Danny and I refurbished this area a couple of years ago to give us more room, and I fucking love it; every damn day.

The far wall is 6 feet long and consists of 2 windows that take up most of the wall; frosted to ensure no one can see in, but still gives a lot of natural light. The bottom 18 inches is a solid, gray stone bench that stretches the entire length of the wall. The two side walls are filled with the same gray stone used in the bench to give it a cohesive look. Then, the pièce de résistance, or pieces really, are the two 20-inch rainfall systems. Each has its own panel on the wall closest to it, with multiple stream settings and LED options. Whether we want to shower together or separately, need a pressure massage, or a light, calming shower, we have it covered.

Since we didn't want to block the view, we closed the area with a long glass wall and a single, extra-wide glass door. I step in and start pushing buttons. Maybe a hot, hard, pulsating shower will help relieve the ache in my muscles; and in my heart.

The jets hit me from all sides, pounding into the muscles in my back and sides better than any massage chair could. Leaning my forehead against the thick glass wall, I take in a deep breath. Steam fills my lungs and floods my veins as I close my eyes and try my damnedest to get those big, blue eyes out of my mind.

Groaning, I squeeze my eyes to the point of pain before hauling my body up and backing away from the wall. I swipe my Canyon soap and lather it angrily between my hands. With more force than necessary, I clean the sweat from my body, rinse quickly, and then, squirting far too much shampoo into my palm, begin lathering my hair. I scrub so viciously that my scalp prickles with pain. An agonized growl tumbles out of me as I rinse my hair out.

My phone rings out, successfully pulling me out of my tortuous mind. With a heavy breath, I shake my head, hoping to clear my thoughts and begin conditioning my hair. The ringing ends and immediately starts up again; pushing me to rush through my beard cleaning.

Pressing a few buttons on the panel, I shut off the shower, then step out onto the heated floors. My phone pings with a notification, and I grumble at the disturbance. *Jesus. What's the damn hurry?*

Swiping a towel from the hook, I barely dry myself off before tucking the towel around my waist. I pick up my phone and glance at the two missed calls. Both are from Charlie; the unofficial leader of our little team, who is currently away on assignment.

Sighing heavily, I step out of the bathroom and into my room, calling Charlie and clicking the phone over to speaker.

The phone rings out, and he answers just as I reach my dresser.
"E. Got news. Oasis tonight at cricket's ring."
With a click, he's gone.

I dress quickly, running the towel through my hair. As I jog back to the bathroom, I quickly finger-comb my long hair, then toss the towel in the hamper. After combing my hair with an actual comb, I rub some beard oil into my beard. I don't have time to balm it since we have to get going now. It will take us just under two hours to get to the meeting location near La Porte

Rushing out of the bathroom, I run straight into Danny. We collide with a garbled "Oomph" and barely remain upright. Danny chuckles, as he asks, "Where's the fire, Love?"

I feel heat flood my cheeks and know that I really need to get my shit together. Clearing my throat, I barely manage a slight grin before shaking my head. "Sorry. Uh, we have a meeting tonight."

Danny's face immediately turns serious. With a nod, he turns on his heel and runs out of the room. Knowing he's going to grab his favorite knives and shove them in every available hiding place brings a genuine smile to my face. *My sweet, little, psychopath.*

Feeling my smile grow, I realize that I'm finally breathing normally. Satisfied that my head is in the right space to do my damn job, I grab my phone from the dresser and head out of the room to get Stu.

Hopefully, Charlie finally gets to come home for a bit. His last mission has kept him away for almost three weeks. And we could really use him to reel us all back in. Because, right now, shit is fucked.

~CHAPTER 13~

Beatrice

This last week has been painfully boring. I sat in more meetings this week than I have in the last four weeks combined. As soon as I logged off of my last meeting, I was ready to heat up my leftover lo mein and down a bottle of Fireman's #4 Blonde Ale.

Deciding on music instead of a movie, for now, I walk over to my record player. Unlatching the lid, I open it, then turn to browse the assortment of records I've collected lined up on the shelf. Corrine Bailey Rae calls out to me, so I carefully slide the vinyl out of the record sleeve and put it on the platter. Already knowing where the third track starts, I turn the tonearm, carefully set the stylus down, then push power. Put Your Records On slowly plays through the speaker and a small sense of peace settles me.

Grabbing my dinner from the kitchen, I amble to the living room and plop onto my oversized, round swivel chair. Sitting my dinner on the side table, I grab my gray, weighted hoodie blanket and slip it on. Burrowing in, I inhale deeply as my eyes close. One by one, I feel every muscle in my body slowly relax.

Reaching over, I take a huge gulp of my beer before swapping it for my food.

The light, freeing lyrics of the song helps me let go of the crazy shit from the last week: The way E made my body light up like a thousand fireflies buzzing through me; how Stu brought me out of my flashbacks and wrapped me comfortably in his arms; my hormones going crazy around Danny, Even, and Stu last weekend; my impromptu video session with Alpha...

I just... I just need to refocus, pack up all of these stupid hormones and emotions into a little tiny box and light it on fire.

Shaking my head, I try to clear my thoughts and focus on the music filtering through my space. I take a long pull from my beer before grabbing my plate and showing a mouthful of lo mein straight into my hole. No need to be polite and crap when I'm by myself.

All.

By.

Myself.

Exhaling heavily, I down the rest of my beer and toss my noodles on the side table. *I know exactly what I need.*

Flipping through my phone, I click on the app I need. I'm technically not ready to take on my next target, but there's no reason I can't have a little fun beforehand. Usually, I meet an app guy *after* I nab my target, and want to expel my adrenaline before waking him.

But, I'm feeling, off, I guess. I don't know, but I need to get my head on straight.

For the next ten minutes, I scroll through my matches and try to figure out the top three I want to contact. Of course, E is there, but I can't see him again. I don't think. At least, not now.

We crossed one of my hard lines by kissing, and I don't think it's wise to meet again.

Ugh, I'm irritating myself with all these wishy-washy girly feelings.

Taking a deep breath, I randomly pick a guy. Scanning to make sure most of our hard lines and preferences seem aligned, I send a message. I usually prefer to talk for a few days to a couple of weeks, ensuring we have similar expectations for our meeting. But, tonight, I don't care. I just need... *a release*.

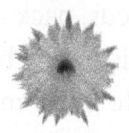

J should be here any minute. After a few short and sweet messages, I decided to invite him to the back of the property. It's large enough that he won't be anywhere near my actual residence. In fact, I'm technically inviting him to another address altogether; something that took me years to pull off.

My entire property is 10 acres. However, my main house is in the middle of my favorite four-acre section, complete with a little creek and the best paths to run my four-wheeler. I have that properly fenced off, whereas the other two sections have bland barbed-wire fencing surrounding them. Each has its own address and "houses" that get plenty of junk mail. That way, to anyone else, it appears to be three separate properties owned by different people. At least, that's what the public documents say.

The other two pieces of my property are split almost 50/50 into about 3 acres each. The one I'm not using tonight has a small trailer on it—nothing fancy—that I use to "get away" sometimes. I've painted almost every surface—random doodles, splatter paint. Whatever I want, when I want.

The section I'm currently on is the most densely covered area. Where the other small section has a large clearing and a decent-sized pond, this slice of heaven is trees, trees, and more trees. An array of deciduous trees ranges further than the eye can see in any direction. Most of them have been here for hundreds of years and have nice, large trunks that I can easily find refuge behind; and sometimes in. The gravel driveway is only about half a mile long and is the only thing that isn't blanketed by grass and, you guessed it, trees.

This house was the original one on the property when I first bought it. It's cute, simple, and almost cottage-like. It's very different from the trailer and the log-chic house that I actually reside in. This one reminds me of my grandmother.

Worn brick surrounds the exterior except for light-colored wood trim. A single large window in the front is shuttered by two large wooden shutters that match the trim. The door is nothing to write home about. It's a simple wooden door with a peephole and also matches the little bit of wood trimming the edges of the house. On each side of the house is a singular, small window. Shortly after moving in, I upgraded all the locks and hinges since they were the originals and not secure at all.

The roof above the front door extends about 8 feet over the front deck in a triangular shape, and the furthest end is held up by two large columns made up of thick wooden beams that... match the house's trim.

Honestly, it's not much to look at. Even the deck is made up of the same colored wood used to trim the house.

Inside isn't much better. I tore out all of the 50s-style wallpaper. Why so many women enjoyed roses plastered on everything is beyond me. I may be cynical, but I *hate* roses- always have. They are way too expensive and way too predictable. *Boring.*

So, yeah, I tore that all right out before I even moved in. I painted the walls a nice, soft cream color, threw in a few pieces of antique furniture I bought at an auction, and lightly decorated them. *Very* lightly. I knew this wasn't going to be my forever spot, and I already had big plans for the log house I wanted to build, so I made this my temporary dwelling. Upgraded what needed to be upgraded and left the rest to nature. Now, I really only use this on the rare occasion when someone wants to come over. I don't like people being in my space. I know all too well how quickly your personal space can be tainted...

My phone pings with a notification just as I begin to swirl down a dangerous memory. *Thank God.*

Opening the kink app, I click on the message from J.

J: 3 minute ETA.

Me: Awesome! Just look for the mailbox with the galaxy racoon. The dirt road will wind a bit, then you'll see the little house. My little gray Civic is parked on the right.

I drove my little car here, not wanting him to be able to track my SUV or something. I didn't have enough time to vet "J" like I usually would have, so I took a few precautions. I almost never use this old car, so there's no way he'd recognize it out and about.

With a deep breath, I check to make sure that the only light on is the one on the porch. Then, I make my way into the bathroom to put on my mask. I felt way too exposed with E so I told

J I would wear the mask. I may very well do it every time now. Hopefully, it will help keep the boundary firmly in place.

Slipping on my black Venetian party mask, I clip the band to my hair on both sides of my head. I am really excited to wear this one because it's a full-face mask, only showing my eyes and a little bit of my forehead. It's almost butterfly-shaped, with how it dips down from the top on both sides and meets just above my nose. The black material is thin and breathable. On the right side of the mask are little fabric flowers flowing down. The eyes are each rimmed with little rhinestones, which help my blue eyes pop. The left side is covered in an intricate black lace with no further additions. The nostril cut-outs are just large enough that I should have good airflow, and I'm more than certain that I won't have any breathing problems as I test the heaviness of the fabric across the mouth. Finally, a singular flower is affixed to the bottom where my mouth is, so there should be no room for mistakes this time.

With a final check, I tousle my fingers through my hair to fluff it up a bit. The mask totally completes the look and comes off as something sexy yet sinister. Twisting a little, I begin to second-guess my decision to give in so easily to his choice of clothing. I feel a lot more exposed than I like. He wanted a simple blank tank top with a black, flowy skirt. The skirt is adorable, but the tank makes me feel like a sausage exploding from its casing. *Not cute.*

He tried to tell me to wear heels, but, *pfft,* yeah, right. Instead, I'm donning my trusty Chucks.

Every part of me is smooth, silky, and desperately ready to be played with. Checking my phone one last time, I activate the alarm parameters I've set up for every 'encounter.' One can never be too careful. My system blinks before turning green, letting me know that it's running; then, the alarm immediately begins counting down from 90 minutes.

I know me, and I know how long these things take. If I don't deactivate the alarm or reset it using my own complicated pin, all of the information I have on this person, including any images or videos my security system catches, will be sent directly to Stu. Not that he knows that. But, unfortunately, he's all I've got.

Which is yet another reason why I need this dingus to hurry up and get any further more-than-friendly ideas about Stu out of my head.

As soon as I click out of the security app, my phone dings.

> J: Ready to play hide and seek?

I feel adrenaline surge through my body, my clit playing its own little happy tune, as a smirk forms across my face.

Shutting off all of the lights, I slip out the back door. We agreed that that message would be the code so I would know when he reached the mailbox, giving me plenty of time to hide.

> Me: Start counting...

With that, I turn off the sound, shove my phone in my bra, and slip into the night.

~CHAPTER 14~

Stu

The ride to our meeting was uncomfortably tense. I'm not mad at Even, per se, I'm just hurt- no, shocked- I guess. I've been dreaming and wanting and hoping for Bea for so damn long.

I didn't know she was even 'entertaining' hook-ups. I mean, not that it's a bad thing, women can do whatever they want but, *fuck*. Maybe I would have asked her out or something had I even had an inkling that she was down. *Maybe. Probably not.* Ok, I wouldn't have because I want it all; her all. She's clearly just... playing? I've shared women with the guys before, but I don't know, it's Bea. Sweet, quiet, hurting Bea.

"...these bastards have been meeting women all over. Rapes them within an inch of their lives, then writes whatever disgusting slur about their physical appearance they feel describes them, before leaving them on their doorstep." Charlie's beastly growl breaks me out of my head and forces me to focus back on our meeting.

"How do you know this is the guy? Or guys?" Even asks, combing through the data we pulled up on our tablets.

Charlie leans over and clicks a few buttons before a new window on the screen opens. "All of the women used various online apps to talk with just one of them. Same stories: one male, sweet, charming, you know..." He shakes his head with a shrug before sighing heavily. "But, the women all say more than one man showed. And, they all had something in common..."

I have barely finished reading the data before Danny chimes in, "Role play?"

Charlie nods, his stern voice clipped as he says, "Not just any role play." He clears his throat, but before he can continue, Even grits through his teeth, "Primal play! He's turning their desires into actual fear?!" Even bangs the wooden table we're sitting at, hard enough that it vibrates through the rest of us. Of course, he's pissed. Even likes primal play, a lot. But he's also a pleasure Dom. I've lived with them long enough to know and understand that Even would never willingly hurt someone unless it brings them pleasure.

But, even he has limits.

I look over at Danny to see how he's handling this; knowing this is probably beating him down, too. Danny always has a hard time with the cases about women being mutilated. He was forced to watch his mother tortured and killed because of his piece of shit sperm donor.

His eyes are laser-focused, and his breathing is steady and perfect. If you didn't know better, you would have no idea that Danny's beast is in charge right now. But, we can tell. The way his pocket knife travels across his knuckles, and the way his eyes have darkened as he probably pictures the hell he wants to rain down on these men, are his only outward tells.

My laptop pings in front of us, causing me to flinch and Danny to scowl. Charlie raises a brow and nods his chin, silently commanding me to check the alert.

It was easier to just bring my laptop and start running trackers while we combed through information on the tablets. I have so many applications running that I'm surprised my system hasn't fried. Crimson Knights, Bea, this asshat, and about a dozen others.

I click on the little notification panel on the bottom right of my screen and my eyes widen. "Fucking dumbass. We've got 'em!" I exclaim, tapping the screen a little harder than I should.

Twirling the laptop around so everyone can see, I explain, "I knew this guy was probably bouncing his IP address all over the place so I had the system track patterns, hoping I could get into a back door. I also narrowed down parameters for male app users for various dating or hookup sites." With another click, I bring up the next page. "There's his IP address. He just logged on."

Charlie looks up at me; the hope we can catch these guys soon hanging heavy in the air. He doesn't even need to say the words. With a nod, I turn the laptop back around and begin clackin' away. I can feel everyone's heavy stares boring into me but I live for this. Following little cookie crumbs back to the big bad wolf's house. No one talks. No one moves. With the exception of the waves crashing against the shore, there are no sounds. Most people have already left the area in favor of home or bars so, it's just us.

"Fuck yeah!" I exclaim, slamming my hand on the table. "Gotcha, bastard." A few more keystrokes and...

"I've got the new messages. They're meeting tonight."

"Find out who and let's get going. Try to get her info to warn her. Now!" Charlie abruptly stands and takes off for the truck; leaving the rest of us to grab our things and catch up.

If there's a chance, albeit a small one, to save this woman, we have to move fast. I'm walking as fast as I can while balancing my computer on one hand. My other hand dances across the keyboard as I work my way into the app's system to pull up the woman's info.

But, when I click on her profile, I freeze.

All the air whooshes out of me instantly as my brain tries to connect the dots. There are so many dots. It doesn't make sense. It can't b-

"Stu! Fuck! Stu, what is it?" Even must sense something; all the things. I don't fucking know but when he goes to grab my arm to get me to move, my eyes shoot up and meets his gaze.

Four seconds. It takes four seconds for him to see whatever my brain is showing through my eyes.

Charlie honks the horn impatiently but I can't seem to move. It's like I'm frozen in space and time. Even grabs the computer away from me and roughly shoves it into Danny's hands. *When did he get here?*

When he turns to face me, he puts both of his big hands on my shoulders and gently squeezes. "Stu. Whatever it is, we have to go. Now. I need you to snap out of it if we have any chance of saving this girl."

His stern yet gentle voice helps bring me back into my body. I feel tears brimming in my eyes and before I can even share what I learned, Danny roars, "He's meeting fucking Beatrice?! Get in the GODDAMN car, NOW!"

And **that's** what I needed. Danny doesn't curse. Like, almost never. It was the last push I needed to come back to myself. Blinking a few times and shaking my head, I nod and sprint towards the car with Even.

Once all of the doors slam shut, Charlie's gunning it. Danny looks at my computer and rattles off an address I'm not totally familiar with, but it's close to where Bea lives. *Fuck, fuck, fuck.*

Even, who's in the front passenger seat, looks over at Charlie and winces. "We'll drive back and get your bike tomorrow."

Charlie shakes his head in response. "Didn't even think about it. Just knew we had to move." His tone is quiet and deadly; clearly not caring about his bike over the possibility of saving someone.

Even grunts in approval before he turns towards me, locking his eyes on mine. The rage and terror in his eyes mirror the way his body vibrates; like he's physically holding himself back from going off. "Explain." To anyone else, the animalistic growl through his gritted teeth would have probably sounded like an immediate threat of danger. But, I know him better than that. He's in shock, pissed, and very protective over people he cares about. Clearly, Bea already has him wrapped around her finger if he's gone E-Hulk over her.

Danny passes back my computer and I start filling everyone in on what I've found. While we're excited we may catch the guy, we're also *very* aware that we're about an hour and a half away from the address.

And *he's* supposed to be there in an hour.

~CHAPTER 15~

Beatrice

A little shiver of anticipation runs down my spine as I make my way through the woods. The further I get from my little cabin, the darker it gets. Dusk has come and gone, and I'm surrounded by the symphony of the nightlife around me. I'm not running. Not yet. Just taking a brisk walk until I find the perfect spot to stop and wait.

I like this game. A little hiding, a little seeking, a little rough action from a man that's been vetted thoroughly by the only app I will ever use to find a nighttime playdate. It's all in good fun, and it may or may not help me forget some of the bad memories. The ones where I didn't have a choice. The ones that grip me by my throat while I'm sleeping and squeeze until I pray for the sweet release of death; only to wake up and realize that I'm still very much alive.

I step behind a massive oak tree and lean against it. For a brief moment, I look up at the stars. Tonight is so clear and utterly perfect. I'm far enough away from major shopping centers and highways that I can see *everything*.

A serene smile pulls my mouth up as I spot the Big and Little Dippers, and then move on to find Polaris, the North Star. Something about looking up into the night sky always gives me a deep feeling of tranquility.

Breathing in deeply, I close my eyes and focus for a moment on the nocturnal sounds around me. Grasshoppers and crickets play a rhythmic tune while an owl nearby hoots out his own melody. A gentle breeze blows through the trees and I feel my hair move around my shoulders under the strap of my mask.

Snap-Crunch-Crinch!

The sounds coming from behind me startle me enough that I bite my tongue when I jump.

My heart rate picks up, and my smile widens as I realize that my friend is here to play. Adrenaline courses through my veins and I duck low for a moment, straining my ears to pick up his general speed and direction. But, what I don't expect is multiple sounds coming from the same direction.

Closing my eyes, I focus everything I have on listening to the footsteps coming from the direction of the cabin.

Thunk

"Shit."

"Shut up, Dumbass."

Durnit! We did *not* agree to more than one player. As I consider my next move, anger and fear fight for dominance and my blood boils.

I can hear them shuffling closer to me and I stop second-guessing. This is my house, my property, my rules.

With a shift on my heel, I sprint through the trees where I know I have a pile of debris I've been working on. We had a bad storm a couple of weeks ago so I made huge piles of downed limbs and never got around to finishing this section. I was *supposed* to finish the cleanup and burn it last weekend, but I was apparently delirious from lack of touch and went way off the rails. Broken limbs may not be the best defense, but I'd rather have something if I need to fight back.

I'm already panting from a mix of running and pure adrenaline but I send up a "thanks" to anyone listening that I can breathe perfectly through the mask. My arms pump as my legs carry me through the trees until I finally reach the clearing. I'm immediately filled with relief when I spot the huge pile of broken limbs standing tall and proud; like a beacon of hope. Hopefully, I won't need to defend myself. But then again, he brought someone without my permission, so I'm not getting the sense that he's very respectful.

"Here, kitty, kitty," A nasally male voice calls out. It sounds creepy and I instantly visualize a 40-year-old, slimy man with a 70s porn 'stache and beady little eyes. Ok, I may be projecting because I loathe the pet name "Kitty." It grosses me out almost as much as a man asking me to call him "Daddy." I have issues, but... ew, I just can't.

However, I don't yuck anyone's yum. If that's their thing, so be it. Just don't involve me.

I round the backside of the large pile of debris and slip down into the sloped pit I dug out a few years ago for controlled burns. Right as I get to the bottom, my shoe gets caught between two large limbs. I yank and pull as quietly as I can, but also keeping in mind that one wrong move and this whole, big fricking pile will come down on my head. Not what I had in mind for tonight... or ever, really.

Finally, I unstick my foot and quickly search for a branch that may be useful if needed.

"Come out, little kitty. We won't bite." That voice sounds more gravelly than the last. But, something else in his tone causes my whole body to erupt in goosebumps. Whatever it is, I don't want it.

After a few cuts and scrapes to my arms, I finally find a worthy piece. It's a Post Oak branch that is just heavy enough to cause damage but not so heavy that I can't wield it with one hand. Part of the tip is jagged from where the branch was broken free from the tree. It's not as good as my knives, but it'll do.

Turning, I quickly make my way out of the pit, ducking down just on the outer edge. The tree line is too far and I can tell from their steps they have already entered the clearing.

"Pink Unicorn!" I scream.

That's it. Safeword is out there. Scene is done.

"Awww, Kitten," the gravelly voice chides. His voice drips in condescension masked by playfulness. "It's too soon. We haven't even played yet."

And, just as I feared, this isn't a scene; it's a trap.

Forking donkey balls! I know better than to not do my own vetting. But noooo. Little Miss Hussy Pants got her tubes in a twist thinking about the guys from last weekend that I just had to jump the gun.

I mentally blow a raspberry as I finish yelling at myself. I really do know better. I mean, geez, how many times does a girl need to be attacked or taken advantage of before she learns her lesson... or the universe says it's enough?

Using every ounce of willpower I have, I force my voice to stay firm as I answer. "Sorry, not sorry. We didn't agree to add anyone to the scene. I'm no longer comfortable so we are done." I try to inject as much confidence and strength in my voice as possible. I mean, I know the app will check on him but, dang, I really screwed up this time.

"We'll make it worth your while." The nasally one comments through the clearing. I can hear their footsteps, one set on each side of the pit, but the gravelly voice is closest.

The other guy's voice gets darker and more sinister the closer he gets. "Besides, you're the one who likes this. Chasing, capturing..." I position my body towards the direction of his voice. It's so dark and my ears are ringing so loudly that I can no longer hear their footsteps.

With my branch out in front of me, like the sword I wish it was, I begin backing away from the pit, towards the tree line. I may very well have to run for it. But, crap noodles, I am *not* built for that.

"...Taking." The last word is whispered into my ear just as two long arms clamp around my chest, pulling me into a warm body.

A shrill scream leaves my throat and I immediately thrash my head back, praying to catch this jackhole in the nose. Unfortunately, he's a little smarter than I hoped, as he pushes his head down until the top of his head basically rests on the top of my back; right where it meets my neck. He pulls me closer to him, and the pressure from his hard head digging into the top of my spine causes me to cry out in pain.

A low tutting of disapproval filters through my ears as I wrestle the bastard behind me. Smashing my heel down, I connect with something hard and unmoving.

"Steel toe boots. Very effective." The man in front of me says casually with a grin.

I can barely see his eyes, but I can sure feel them. The darkness within them flows out like an inky aura of death and carnage.

Shivers cause my body to tremble and my breaths start coming in harsh pants. My body hurts from exertion laced with fear and my brain isn't able to make a clear path of action. It's like my brain is shutting itself down; preparing for what's to come.

The man in front of me steps closer and I wave the branch in a futile attempt to make contact. The man behind me has a solid grip around my upper body, so the limb is now completely useless.

It's then I realize he must have readjusted his head, as it now leans up against the right side of mine; like he's a lover holding me tightly. *Gag.*

Something hard pokes me in my back and I quickly realize it's the creeper's little pocket pal. *Ew.*

"Looks like we've got ourselves a fat little kitty, huh, Drew?" the obvious leader says, raking his eyes over my body. Without a cloud in the sky, there's enough moonlight to get general figures and shapes. But I definitely can't tell you what this jackhole looks like—other than maybe 5'9" with a medium build. The guy behind me is a touch taller but slimmer. Other than that, I can't see a dang thing.

Something wet and slimy hits the bottom of my neck on the right side. It takes only a moment to realize that it's his tongue. I try to pull away as it travels up my neck before flicking my ear back and forth; slobbering on it like a Bulldog.

"I like fat kitties." He wheezes. It briefly makes me wonder if he has asthma or if he just naturally sounds like a sick perv.

"Get the hell off me," I gag. It may or may not be fake. "Your breath smells like you licked a skunk's butthole." I look over at the leader, nodding my chin at him, "Or maybe he licked yours. Either way, one of you needs to see a doctor because GROSS!"

I know I'm pissing them off and I don't care. This may be my last night on Earth but they sure as hell aren't going to have me just roll over and play dead. Nope. Not this girl. Never again.

A growl vibrates through the man's chest behind me and he bites down on the top of my right shoulder. It feels like his teeth are scraping across the bone, and I scream out in pain; vaguely feeling the blood trickle down my arm and chest. I clearly hit a nerve and definitely didn't peg him for a vampire. *Cheese-its!*

As soon as the thought leaves my head, warmth, and pain explode across my right cheek. Stars spark through my vision and my neck pops from the force.

It takes a few seconds for my brain to come back online. But, by that point, I'm being twisted around and shoved to my back. The back of my head hits the ground with a dull *thud* and my breath is painfully forced from my lungs from the impact. I'm still trying to blink away the spots in my vision. My eyes water as sand and dirt swirl around my face, and I pant and heave for breath.

Suddenly, it's like a telescope zooms *way* into my situation; like in a movie. I see everything that's going on and everything that will probably happen. And that's all I needed.

I finally snap back away from the pain. I've done this before. Separate the pain, block it out, deal with it later. *If there is a later.* Until then, fight like hell.

I start to thrash, squirm, scream, flail... at one point, a hand tries to cover my mouth, and I chomp on it like I'm a friggin' piranha. When that hand rips away from my mouth, a solid body *thumps* down on top of my thighs. My hands form fists, and I fight with everything I have; praying to connect. A grunt of pain and a shout of "Fuck!" greets me, and I smile wide, allowing that little bit of progress to fuel my continued rage.

"Get her under control!" A voice barks from somewhere behind my head. A thin, clammy hand wraps around my left wrist and mashes it backward to the ground above my head. My eyes widen as the movement causes Mr. Wheezer to come ridiculously close to my face. It also has the terrible effect of causing my back to arch and my breasts to mash into his chest.

The moonlight is just enough to see the anger coursing through his eyes. His stomach-curdling breath fans across my face repeatedly and causes hot bile to surge up into my throat.

His free hand reaches behind him as he sneers, "I've got something to shut her up."

And that's the opening I need.

My right hand comes up the second his hand disappears behind his back. In a move I've had to use before, unfortunately, I hook my thumb into his nostril, press my pointer finger into the corner of his left eye and squeeze. I feel my thumbnail embed itself into his nostril, giving me a good anchor to use the rest of my fingers to dig in behind his eye.

His answering roar is a glorious hymnal as he immediately drops my other wrist and rears back. *Stupid boy.*

I use his lack of balance and, obvious surprise, to buck my hips upwards. I still have a pretty good hold of his eye and nose as his body lurches forward over me. Unfortunately for him, the sudden movement forward causes my fingers to dig even deeper into his socket; effectively popping out the gooey little organ.

Taking advantage of his position, I wrap my legs around his scrawny butt. When our hips are pinned together, I use my left hand to push his shoulder diagonally backward and flip our positions.

With a thud and a scream of agony, he hits the ground. He flails about; clasping his face and wailing loudly. I quickly clamber off of him and shakily stand before realizing that his eye is firmly-or should I say squishy- in my hand. *Holy crackerballs. I pulled his eye all the way out!*

For a brief moment, I watch in fascination as he flops around and screams like a maniac. But, that proves to be one moment too long.

"You fucking bitch!" The other guy was noticeably absent during my tussle and I forgot he was even here. *Idiot.*

I don't have time to react before a hard body slams right into my back, sending me flying down into the debris pit. Pain courses through my body as I belly-flop to the ground. The sound of limbs and branches collapsing around us and down the other side of the pile echoes out through the night. The air is knocked out of me and I start gasping and coughing for breath.

I'm still wheezing and groaning for air when something yanks me up by my hair; forcing me to crawl over branches on all fours to prevent being scalped. My knees barely hit solid ground before the hold on my hair loosens just in time for two large hands to engulf my wrists and wrench them behind me. *Holy shit. He moved fast.*

My breathing is gurgled and painful as cold metal cinches around each wrist behind my back. With a rough shove, I face-plant into the sloping side of the debris pit, spluttering and choking against the dirt.

"Fucking ugly ass, fat bitch! You think you're better than me?!" I don't have time to even attempt a witty comeback before he's kicking me in the ribs hard enough that I roll onto my side.

My mask is completely sideways on my face; cutting off my ability to see with my left eye and greatly impeding the right. Sparklers filter through my vision as my body tries to combat the pain with adrenaline. The man behind me roars as he flips me from my side to my back, squishing my cuffed hands underneath me, and causing my shoulder to dislocate with a loud *pop*.

"...easy. But, no... had to be..." The man is mumbling out an angry monologue of curses as my knees bear his weight and he rips my tank down the middle. The pain in my knees is excruciating and I fear they may snap backward from the pressure. My overactive imagination also wonders if my lower spine could break from being smashed against my bound hands.

I vaguely feel a cool breeze on my thighs as my skirt is moved around and my panties are unceremoniously ripped away. But, pain trumps everything for a moment. It's too painful to breathe, or fight, or scream. Everything throbs and aches and my body has no idea what to focus on.

Until two fingers are jammed deep inside me. The burning sensation rips a loud, screeching sound from my throat. "That's it," he growls. "Figures a fat chick like you would have a tight kitty," He grits between his teeth.

My brain finally decides to be helpful as it begins to flood my body with numbness. As I begin zoning out, I'm momentarily grateful that his fingers leave my body and hope he's done with me. Maybe he'll just kill me now and get it over with.

Then, I hear him spit.

~CHAPTER 16~

Danny

We pull up at a tiny, little cabin that makes me think of my mother. Small, cute, tidy, and sweet-looking. She would have loved a place like this. A sharp pang in my chest has me absently rubbing it as we quietly step out of the car. Once we hit the gravel drive, we turned off the headlights, hoping not to force the bastards' hands into hurting Beatrice.

Oh, sweet Bea. You can tell she doesn't laugh or smile much, so when she does, it shines brighter than the sun. We only spent about an hour with her, but you can learn a lot about a person just by observing them. The shadows in her eyes called to a darkness in my soul.

She puts on a comfortable, confident front but is neither of those things unless she can control every aspect of a situation. That alone tells me all I need to know about some of her "life experiences."

Knowing the little bit I do about her, I can see why she doesn't trust easily, if at all, and prefers to be alone- because she's the only person in her life who doesn't let her down. Her heart is locked up tighter than Fort Knox, but she cares deeply for others, even those she doesn't know. She has a gentleness about her that makes me want to comfort her, snuggle her, and take care of her. And I rarely feel that way.

Hell, I was surprised when I was immediately possessive of Even, Charlie, and Stu, but those were more "Bro" feelings; guys I could go into a dangerous situation with and feel safe. And those relationships were, and are, fostered by our mutual hatred of assholes who take advantage of others; especially women and children.

Of course, those feelings morphed a lot more between Even and me. What can I say, I love the big guy. We are basically the opposite in every way. He's big and scary-looking but soft and gooey on the inside. Always willing to be the first in the face of danger and stopping at nothing to ensure people's safety.

As for me, I look sweet and innocent. Semi-charming, really goofy. But, I'm the darkest of our group. I'm the interrogator, the torturer, the executioner; and I fucking love it.

But the moment I met Bea, I knew she'd be ours- ours to care for, ours to protect, ours to love.

A loud, very male, roar of agony penetrates through the trees, causing us all to freeze for a second. Then, like the team we fucking are, we all take off in a sprint past the back of the house. As my arms and legs fill with adrenaline, I feel a slow grin form on my face. If that's a male scream, our feisty little Bea's giving him a run for his money. *Good girl.*

My cock hardens in my pants as the thought of violence flows through me. If there's anything left of these assholes by the time I get there, I'm definitely going to have some fun.

I groan under my breath as images of Bea and I "playing" together flip through my mind. We could take turns slicing and dicing our dear friends. And, if she needs a little extra stress relief, well, I can handle that, too.

My filthy thoughts are interrupted by a strange sound. It's almost like a bunch of logs or something falling in the woods. The fuck? A quick glance toward Charlie tells me he's thinking the same; his head tilted like he's confused.

We start slowing down as we see a clearing up ahead. Needing to scout out where Beatrice is, and where our little friends are, we split up: Even and I to the left of the clearing, and Stu and Charlie to the right. The good news is: I only hear one male voice talking, and he sounds pissed. The other male is screaming in agony. The bad news is: I don't hear Bea.

We quickly and as quietly as possible travel a few more feet until we hit the clearing. The moon gives me just enough light to see shadows of a man on the ground, crying and flailing with his hands over his face. In front of him is a huge dirt pit that appears to be filled with broken limbs and branches. "...ass, fat bitch..." Comes from somewhere just out of sight.

And I. See. Red. *I know that motherfucker ain't talking to Bea like that.*

A warm hand presses down on my shoulder just as I take a step to rush in. As I look into Even's eyes, he puts a finger up to signal we need to go in slow because we still don't have Bea in sight. All I can manage is a clipped nod before we breach the clearing and silently head over to the pile of broken trees.

As we round the corner, I see a dark figure hovering on all fours, just inside the pit. But, what I can't see, I hear. Bea's scream of pain lights up every damn nerve I have and there is no stopping me.

Just as I hear a spitting sound coming from the asshole on top of her, I'm barreling into him full-force. Admittedly, it wasn't thought out very well as my shoulder crashes into the bastard's head. But when we land a few feet away in a tangle of limbs and fury, I'm at least relieved I didn't hurt Bea in the process.

Not that I can worry about that right now. Nope. Right now I get to be lost in the red place.

~CHAPTER 17~

Stu

Charlie and I are just running around the corner when Danny goes flying through the air, lifting the prick off of my girl. Her scream almost brought me to my knees, but thankfully, Charlie moving in front of me reminded me that she still needed us. That it's not too late.

Even's already knocked out the screaming little bitch on the ground and is making his way toward us as I slide into the branch pit. Dirt lifts around me like a fog. I vaguely register that Charlie's helping Danny but all I can see, all I can think about, is Beatrice.

My heart gets caught in my throat as I slow my movements, trying to make sure I don't startle her but desperately wanting to get her away from here. "Bea. Bea, come on. Let's get you home." I try to sound confident and sweet but I can hear the trembling in my voice as my brain unhelpfully shares pictures of what she probably looks like. *Stupid nighttime.*

She doesn't stir. In fact, I'm not sure she's even alive until I put my fingers against her pulse point. It's faint, but it's there.

"Hey Queen Bea, I'm gunna get you out of here. Beatrice? Can you hear me?" My voice trembles with anxiety as I try to rouse her calmly.

I hate myself for touching her without her permission but we've got to go. My breaths are coming in short pants as I notice the pale skin of her legs, thighs, and stomach illuminated by the moon. My stomach lurches at the thought of her being exposed against her will and my eyes fill with tears.

"Stu, we gotta go." Even's calming and authoritative voice brings me out of my panic. With a nod, I tug my shirt off my body and wrap it gently around hers; tucking it behind her as I slide an arm behind her back. Then, I do my best to flip her flowy skirt material down enough to cover her, before sliding my other arm under her knees and lifting her up.

It takes a beat, given the deep slope of the dirt pit we're in, but I finally get us both out. With a quick look around, I see Even has one guy thrown over his shoulder, Charlie has the other guy, and Danny is pacing like a caged animal.

With a whistle from Charlie, we swiftly make our way back through the woods.

My heart is beating out an erratic rhythm in my chest as the woman I've loved for years hangs limply in my arms. As we get closer to the car, I realize that the safest thing to do next is probably going to piss her off. But, she needs help, and we need a safe place to take these assholes.

Dingleberry 1 and 2 get dumped into the trunk as I slide into the back seat with Bea, carefully cradling her head and ensuring all her major parts are covered.

Four doors slamming, one after another, signal we're all ready. Charlie gets his phone out and starts the car. "Doc, we need your help. Meet us at-"

"No!" I yell over him.

Everyone freezes, knowing I never raise my voice or intervene in our leader's decisions. I feel 3 pairs of eyes bore into me as I stare down at Bea and wince, praying my next decision doesn't end our friendship forever.

With a resigned sigh, I look Charlie in the eye and rattle off her address—the one two minutes from where we are, the one she doesn't allow anyone but me in.

Fuck. Please don't hate me, Bea.

Thirty minutes later, we have the Dingleberry twins tied up in Bea's dungeon, and we're all standing around like a bunch of dumbasses in her kitchen, anxiously waiting for Doc's report.

Doc showed up almost fifteen minutes ago. By then, I had laid her on her guest bed, assuming she wouldn't want to taint her own with this mess. Knowing the assholes in the trunk probably won't stay knocked out, I had Danny watch after her as I helped the other two unload the bodies into Bea's dungeon. I could tell Charlie and Even had questions, but it was definitely not the time.

Bea's skin was cold and clammy. She trembled in my arms the whole way here. Once we were in the car, I removed the mask that was sitting sideways on her face; carefully removing the pins in her hair without hurting her further. It was then that I realized her eyes were open. Her breathing was shallow and weak but she was alive. Sort of. It's like she was here physically but completely checked out mentally. I honestly can't tell if that's a good thing or not. Even her panic attacks look different;

like she's just temporarily spaced out. But now, her eyes are dimmer, duller, void of any emotion at all.

Danny's pacing from the kitchen to the living room and back again. Even and Charlie are talking in hushed tones at Bea's little kitchen table, and I'm just leaning against the counter, praying she'll be ok.

I'm about to tell Danny to sit the fuck down because he's driving me nuts but I hear Doc clear his throat as he approaches. All of us instantly rush toward him. Doc lifts a black brow and rubs his salt-and-pepper beard. "I've cleaned her up the best I could. I was able to pop her shoulder back in and put it in a sling. She needed some liquid stitches in a few places on her back from what looked like branches stabbing her but none of them were too terribly deep. Either way, I've left her some antibiotics and pain pills on her nightstand. She's not concussed but has several lumps on her head; none of them needing much more than glue and ice. Her ribs on the left side are cracked and are already bruised, so I wrapped those up for her, but I left the bruise balm on the nightstand, too."

He shifts uncomfortably, darting a look at each of us, looking for God knows what.

"Fuck's sake, Doc, spit it out!" Even's outburst isn't completely unusual, but he's usually much more professional with Doc and Charlie. *Bea really did a number on him, huh?*

Doc levels a look at him causing Even to back down and apologize before rubbing a hand across his face.

Clearing his throat, Doc continues, "The, uh, the bite mark on her shoulder..." He trails off, gauging our reactions. I feel the blood drain from my face and sway a little. None of us are angels, but this is Bea. Sweet, badass, Bea, and this fucker bit her?!

Danny's menacing growl brings my attention back to Doc as he finishes whatever he was saying, "...check in a couple of days to make sure it's healing correctly."

I blink my eyes a few times, having completely missed whatever he said. "She's currently in a dissociative state so I wasn't comfortable with a rape kit-" Again, Danny growls but, this time, Even joins in.

Doc holds up a hand to halt their inner beasts before continuing. "If she wants one, she is free to call or message me, and I'll get the tests run ASAP."

He sighs heavily, likely exhausted by the hour and the circumstance.

"But, I will say, your girl fought hard. Her knees, her knuckles, even her fingers had clear signs of defensive wounds." He chuffs a humorless laugh.

After a brief silence, he frowns, confusion painted across his face. "Were there any liquids there? Not red like blood but something else? Her right hand had a thin layer of a liquid substance I couldn't immediately identify. NOT semen, but not saliva either..."

I frown as I think back to the scene we stumbled upon. I didn't see anything necessarily wet or whatever.

"Eyeball?" Charlie questions. Doc raises his brows in disbelief and intrigue.

Charlie scowls thoughtfully before mumbling, "The guy I knocked out... he was screaming and holding his face before I *silenced* him. When we tied him up in Bea's, uh, *room*," He hesitates, glancing around to determine if he should say more about the "room" our bastard friends are hanging out in. With a gentle shake of my head, I ask him to keep his mouth shut about it.

Clearing his throat, he looks back over at Doc, "Anyways, his whole eye was fuckin' missing and his face was swollen and red.

Even his nose. But, not like she busted it. It was almost like it was stretched and on the same side of his missing eye. I didn't think about it when we tied them up but, is that even possible?"

Silence blankets the kitchen for a long moment as we consider the sweet, sassy woman in the other room potentially being able to do that. I mean, I know what she does in that room. I help her find the assholes to begin with. But, can you pull out someone's eyeball with your bare hands? With her thin, delicate, little hands?

Doc shifts uncomfortably, likely done with all of us and this strange-ass night. "Maybe. It's possible, but it would have to be intentional, with a lot of force. It's really not as easy as people may think."

He sighs heavily and walks over to the sink to wash his hands. Once he's done, he turns around and says, "Well, like I said, if she needs anything, let me know." He levels each of us with a hard glare. Like an overprotective Dad, he's not happy about a woman being mixed up in our violent lives. Little does he know...

Charlie stands to his full height, grasps Doc by the hand, and shakes firmly with a nod. "Thanks, Doc. We've got her." Then he moves and leads Doc out of the kitchen and into the garage.

We're all silently contemplating the turn of events. I vaguely process the closing of the garage door and then the opening and closing of the mudroom door. Heavy, booted footsteps return to the kitchen before stopping somewhere off to my left.

For an eternity, we stand there in silence, staring off into space and thinking about everything that's happened in just a few short hours.

A loud, painful scream cuts through the air, ending our silent reverie. My blood turns to ice but my feet automatically move through the house. Fear zaps through me like lightning bolts and my heart feels like it's going to break through my chest.

I barely cross the threshold of the room before slamming my left hip into a dresser. I dismiss the pain as my eyes quickly scan the room for danger. But, what I see, instead, is painfully familiar. Her body is damn near convulsing, fighting off invisible attackers. Her hair is plastered to her face with sweat and tears.

My body moves on auto-pilot as I kick off my shoes and crawl into her guest bed. Distantly, I can feel the gazes of the other three men as they take in the scene before them, but I don't have time to explain. She's lost in her head and needs help coming back out.

I defensively block her punches and a few kicks as she screams like a banshee. Her face and arms are mottled with bruises but her anguished expression forces me to move faster. Leaning over her, I wrap my arms around her back and plaster my chest to the front of her body. She wails in terror and kicks with all her might, but I plaster myself around her like a spider monkey and turn us so we're lying on our sides.

"Back off!" Danny roars violently. I barely spare them a glance knowing they all look seconds from ripping my dick off and shoving it in my skull.

"I need the heavy blanket. Where's the big, blue blanket?" I scream out, hoping that my voice projects that I not only know what I'm doing, but I fucking need help.

Charlie steps forward and walks to the end of the bed. His brows are furrowed in concentration but heat swirls in his eyes at the possibility that I'm hurting her.

"Charlie, you *know* me. She gets like this sometimes. She needs pressure. Get me the fucking blanket!"

At my harsh tone, Charlie's brows raise comically high, then he shakes his head quickly. Finally, the big doof searches around.

"Not in here!" I bark. "Her room. Across the hall." I motion with my head to make my point, and he and Even quickly move out.

I feel blood trickling down my head where she banged hers against mine. I also know for a fact that my thighs and shins are going to be torn up. One thing about my girl is that she's a fucking fighter. Any other time, it may get me hard, but not when she's like this. *Never* when she's like this.

Even rushes back in with her heavy-ass blanket, grunting with effort. Once he gets to her side of the bed, he struggles with the blanket for a second, before grumbling and lifting it up and over our bodies.

The blanket's heaviness presses us further into the mattress, and I begin softly shushing her, firmly rubbing her back with one hand and gently squeezing the back of her head; making sure I don't press on any bumps. Her face is now pressed up against my neck, just at chest level, and I shutter as I slowly feel her breathing settle.

It takes almost thirty seconds before her upper body relaxes, her arms release the tension she was holding, and her legs finally stop shifting around. Her heart-breaking screams have now lowered to soft whimpers.

Finally, she takes one deep, restorative breath. Then, I feel her snuggle deeper into my chest with a contented sigh.

Knowing she's finally coming down, I lift the pressure from the back of her head and gently run my fingers through her matted hair. I mean, as much as I can. I feel my eyes drift shut as I gently sway us and let everything around us melt away.

When I'm convinced she's finally fallen asleep, I begin to untangle my limbs from around her body; hoping she'll be able to get some sleep. As I lift the blanket off of me from behind, trying to make sure she stays completely surrounded, she sighs sweetly, snuggles deeper into my chest, and purrs quietly, "I love you, Stu. I wish I was good enough..."

Soft snores are the only sounds in the room, and blood whooshes in my ears as I stare down at this crazy, sweet, badass woman and wonder if she meant the words or if she was just dreaming. A wide, dopey grin splits my face as I realize that I don't care. If dream me could make her smile softly and love me like that, maybe the real me could do the same.

Shaking my head out of my own dreams, I look down at her in wonder. Then, I lean over and brush a fleeting kiss on her temple before sliding backward off the bed.

Even looks down at her form from the other side of her bed, and Danny leans against the dresser next to the door. Charlie stands stock-still in the doorway, looking like he's seen a ghost. It's not the worst thing we've ever seen, so I'm not totally sure why he looks like someone just killed his dog.

Filing that nugget away to ask about later, I turn my head and stare at the ceiling. With a heavy sigh, I rub at my chest before scraping my hands through my hair; tugging just a little at the roots. Then, with a final glance at Bea, I nod for the guys to head out.

Quietly, we all file out and I flick the lights off before silently shutting the door behind me.

~CHAPTER 18~

Even

Danny and I plop down on the surprisingly white leather couch. Stu tucks into the giant-ass swivel chair, and Charlie falls into the matching white loveseat by the windows. With a groan, he roughly rubs his hands down in his face then leans his head back on the loveseat, staring up at the ceiling.

"What a fucking mess," He grumbles. With a heavy sigh, he leans forward and braces his forearms on his knees. Staring at the floor for a moment, he begins nodding before looking up at Stu. "Ok, spill."

Stu's eyes shoot up to meet Charlie's gaze. Time stands still as they have a silent conversation. Stu's brows furrow into a deep scowl, and Charlie raises his brow in dominance.

"No, no way," Stu shakes his head adamantly and all but yells. "I will not betray her like that." Since I'm a little closer to Stu, I can see his hands trembling even though the rest of him seems stiff as a board.

Danny shuffles closer to me, intertwining our fingers in my lap and scooching forward on the couch. Little shit loves drama.

I'm mid-eye-roll when Charlie grunts dismissively. His voice is low and menacing as he glares at Stu and delivers each word he speaks with purpose and authority. "I don't give a fuck about betrayal. Right now, we're in some unknown woman's house, who has a fucking dungeon in her garage- and don't think we won't be talking about that, either- who you all clearly know and-" He grunts and waves his hand in there dismissively. "Clearly know or like or are fuckin-"

Stu shoots up off the couch and is in Charlie's space faster than I can blink. A low, rumbling growl fills the silence. When Danny rubs my thigh with his other hand, I realize the growl is coming from me.

Shaking my head out of the daze that is Bea, I look back at Stu squaring off with Charlie. Charlie's standing to his full height, putting him about four inches above Stu, but he doesn't seem bothered by it. In fact, Stu's whole body seems to shift and broaden to match Charlie's much larger, bulkier frame.

With a thin finger, Stu pokes Charlie in the chest. His voice is deeper and, frankly, scarier than I've ever heard it before. "Don't ever talk about her like that again." He grits through his teeth. "She is my friend and you will respect her. She is not a danger to us, or anyone else..." His demeanor shifts slightly as he loses some of his fight. "Well, not to anyone who isn't a soulless, filthy, rat bastard who preys on others."

As he shrugs a shoulder with indifference, I feel my face mirror Charlie's: brows raised high, jaws open in shock. *Did he just insinuate that...*

Stu jumps in again, "And don't think I didn't see the look on your face when you came back to the room. What the hell was that about?!"

"Stu?!" A groggy, pained voice echoes through the living room, ending the remaining standoff between our leader and our hacker. Danny and I bolt upright and see Bea trying to wrap her arms around herself. Her clothes are still torn and tattered. The bruising on her face and arms is more prominent in the light of the living room.

We all stare in shock, not only to see her awake, but to also see her eyes fill with steely determination and a hint of hurt.

Stepping forward, I go to reassure her, but she immediately moves backward, hitting the wall behind her. Squinting at me, she takes in my now dirty clothes, then travels over to Danny, then Charlie, before settling on Stu. This close, I can see the tears forming in her eyes as she looks over at him. "Why are you here? Why did you bring them here? How did y-?"

Stu raises his hands and slowly moves towards her like she's a wounded animal. "Woah, easy Bea." With a glance over his shoulder to Charlie, who nods his permission, Stu turns back and takes another step. "I know you don't know a lot about what I, what we, do..." He gestures to us causing her to flit her eyes over us quickly before landing back on him. "But, we were tracking a guy. A bad guy. And, we found out you two were meeting. What happened tonight..." With a heavy sigh, he drops his hands and furrows his brows in sorrow. "You weren't the first. He's, *they've*, done this before. We tracked him to that property, and got you back here."

I briefly glance over at him and realize that he looks pained. Like it's taking every ounce of restraint he has not to run to her and scoop her into his arms.

The air is still; the silence becomes oppressive as she darts her eyes around the room. Finally, she bites her lip, that plush delicious lip, and softly speaks, "Th-the cuts and stuff. Did you, um-" Her cheek, without the hand-shaped bruise, flushes with embarrassment.

"No. We have a doctor on call. He checked you out. Also said if you wanted tests for, ya know..." He awkwardly flings his hands toward her vagina, and I groan at his sweet but ridiculous inability to talk normally around her. Not that I can blame him.

Her face turns beet red, and her lips begin to tremble. Her voice comes out raspy, likely from her screaming, and so low that we all silently shuffle closer to her. Staring at the ground, she whispers, "So, you found me, saved me, then brought everyone here?"

Stu nods silently, looking at her with worry written all over his body. He kind of looks like a boy who just got sent to the principal's office, and he's scared they're going to call his parents. I'm trying to put the pieces together of their strange dynamic when she interrupts my thoughts.

"Thank you. For your help. But, um, I'm good. You can leave, now."

Danny and I give her gentle smiles and begin to make our way around the couch before Charlie calls out, "We need to grab the other two first. Then we can move out." His whole voice changes from his usually grave tone to something deeper and kind of awkward. *What the hell is going on?*

Bea's eyes grow wide with alarm as she scans the room, assuming she missed who he's talking about. "They're not with us, Queenie. We put them in your *holding* room while Doc checked your injuries." Stu's calm and laid-back response is much closer to his usual demeanor which causes me to relax a little.

But, apparently, that was too soon.

"What?!" Bea screeches indignantly. "Have you lost your ding-dang mind?" Her eyes flash with fury as she stares Stu down. I shuffle a little, the fire in her eyes causing my cock to stir. Images of her sassing me in the forest flash through my mind and I have to actively hold back a moan.

Stu huffs in exasperation, rolling his eyes. "What else were we supposed to do Bea? You were fucking out of it. Danny took out the asshole on top of you and Even had to handle the one-eyed dipshit. And you needed help! This was the closest place we could bring you to get you help as quickly and safely as possible." Stu's pacing like a caged animal; anguish and desperation waft off of him in waves. He tugs his bright pink hair by the roots and growls out.

But, Bea's not backing down. "So you brought a bunch of men, *strangers*, to my place? To *my* dang house and let them see my, my," she flaps her arms towards the garage as she loses her words for a second. Eventually, she huffs out a sigh and rolls her eyes, slapping her hands on her thighs. Then she mumbles, shaking her head angrily, "Figures. Just like every other forking-"

"Don't you dare say I'm like the others! I'm not Matt!" Spittle flies out of Stu's mouth as he releases his emotions. I don't know who the fuck Matt is, but he clearly messed Bea up. And, Stu's so sensitive when it comes to her that if she's trying to compare them, he's going to lose it.

Charlie must sense the same thing as we both step towards them, hoping to de-escalate the situation. But, we don't get far...

Slap! "You son-of-a-jackal! How dare you. Just because you didn't use your friend status to guilt-trip me into fucking you doesn't mean you didn't betray me. How dare you use that against me!"

What. The. Fuck.

~CHAPTER 19~

Beatrice

My whole body is shaking with rage and embarrassment. Here I am, in my dang house, with my only friend, two of his friends, and some other stupidly hot guy. And, yet again, I'm reminded why I don't trust anyone. *Especially* men.

Angry tears stream down my face, making me feel even worse, even more raw and exposed. "Get out. I'll take care of the guys, just... get out." I mumble, staring down at my bare feet. I'm still covered in dirt, my skirt is in tatters, and my slashed-open tank top smells awful. Like dirt, fear, and humiliation.

I hear Stu's heavy, pained sigh as he steps towards me. Holding my hands up, I shake my head, not making eye contact. I know if I do, whatever is in his eyes will break me. And I'm so tired of being broken. So. Damn. Tired.

"Go," I whisper; squeezing my eye shut.

When no one moves to leave, I clear my throat and glance at each of the stupidly handsome men filling my living room, my safe space. I inject as much confidence and conviction as I can before lifting my head completely, chin up, shoulders back. "I appreciate your help. Thank you. But, I've got it from here. I'm going to get cleaned up but when I come out, you all need to be gone."

With that, I turn on my heel and walk over to my room, slamming it closed before all but jogging to the bathroom. Once I close that door, I lean my forehead against it and suck in deep breaths. A sob rips from my throat as my vision tunnels and I collapse on the floor.

Goosebumps litter my skin as Matt leans over me. "I'm your best friend, right?"

I furrow my brows, confused about his question. "Well, yeah. Of course. But,"

He tsks at me, lifting my chin with his finger. "No buts, Beatrice. We're either best friends or we're not."

Clearing my throat I nod. "Yes, we are." I barely whisper.

"Good, and best friends help each other, right?" He implores, his eyes boring deep into mine.

"Y-yes."

With a nod, he smirks and stands back to his full height. "Good. I'm your best friend. And I'm going to help you out."

I feel like I've entered the twilight zone. "What are you talking about?" I'm beginning to think he's sick. He has never acted like this before.

"You're still a virgin, and I'm your best friend, so I'm going to help you out. We both know that I'm the only guy who will give you the chance. I mean, I don't care that you're fatter than most girls. But, you definitely don't want to be the only one in our school who graduates with your virginity. I mean, college is hard. And, not being as pretty as the other girls already puts you at a disadvantage. The last thing you want is also to be considered a prude virgin. Right?"

My brows have hit my hairline as I take in his oddly calm demeanor while he spews this insanity. I mean, sex? Really?! He knows what happened when I was a kid. He knows I'm scared. Why is he really doing this?

Suddenly, I start cracking up. Tears fall from my eyes as I struggle to catch my breath. "Oh my God! You had me, you doofus. Get dressed. I'll buy breakfast," I say, shaking my head and moving to stand.

But, Matt doesn't move out of my way. He puts his hands on my shoulders and gently presses me back down. "You said we were best friends. This is what best friends do. Don't you trust me?" He asks in his sweet little way, his smile tilting into a small smirk.

"Of course I trust you but-"

He silences me with a finger to my lips. "That's all I need to hear. Now, lie back."

Gasping for breath, I blink out of my nightmare. It takes me a few moments to gather myself as my surroundings start to sharpen through the dreamy fog.

I groan as I stretch, realizing I must have fallen asleep on the floor, curled up in the corner between the door and the side wall. I wipe the sweat off my brow and run my free hand through my matted hair. The sling around my other arm is still secured but reminds me of the men I threw out.

Trembling with exhaustion from the night, plus the nightmare of one of the worst betrayals I've ever lived through, I move to stand; grunting as my knees scream at being bent for so long. I fling of the sling, wincing as I squeak out from the pain.

Moving to the shower, I turn it as hot as it can go, then step in. It's not a large shower as it barely fits my plump body. But, it works.

I just stand there, clothes still on, and begin to replay the night. From beginning to ending.

My head thumps against the tiled wall, and I let it all out—all of it. My tears stream like a rushing river, mixing and swirling with the pitter-patter of the water spraying from the nozzle. Eventually, the water runs cold, signaling my need to move. Pushing back the emotional pain, for now, I strip off my clothes, unwrap the bandages tied around my chest, and quickly shampoo and condition my hair; painfully finding more than a few bumps on my head. Once I rinse it all out, I viciously begin cleaning myself with my body wash. It causes the smattering of scratches and minor stitches to sting but I don't have it in me to care. My ribs and shoulder ache painfully, causing my vision to double, but I push through and scrub until I physically can't scrub anymore.

Turning off the water, I step out. The cold floor shocks me so I hurriedly tip-toe to the bathroom cabinet, fling it open, and pull out a fresh towel.

After re-wrapping my ribs and smothering ointment and bruise balm across my body, I swipe the pill bottles sitting on the nightstand. Everything hurts, and I still have work to do. So, I uncap the bottles, chug half a bottle of water before downing the pills, and turn to head out. I don't bother with the sling since I'm going to need to use my arm, but I can't help but flinch as I think about how much this next part is going to hurt.

Three minutes later, I'm stepping into my little garage dungeon, taking in the sight of the two bloody, incapacitated men. The gaping, disgusting hole where the one guy's eye had been causes me to lift my lips in a slight smirk. But, my usual feelings of elation and justice are missing. Now, I'm just...*tired*. No, past tired; I'm utterly and completely exhausted and I'm afraid I've hit my threshold.

An irritated sigh pushes past my lips because I was betrayed by another man, and now I have to get rid of these bozos by myself. All I want to do is curl up in my bed and sleep for a week.

With a sharp exhale, I step past them so I can get to work. I don't even bother waking the two jerks up. Walking behind the one-eyed asshole, I open up my giant toolbox and pull out my Gunny Knife. It's one of my favorite Ka-Bars, and the man who created it is a freaking legend. The cold, smooth handle fits in my palm perfectly. The blade looks like it should be top-heavy, but it's perfectly balanced and perfectly lethal.

With the blade in hand, I come to a stop behind the one-eyed wonder. In a quick movement, I place my hand against his forehead and jerk him back before slitting his throat, ear-to-ear. I step over to his partner and give him the same treatment, and watch as their blood spills out onto the floor.

"Rest in pieces, jackholes," I grumble before shuffling over to the sink to clean my knife. As the water washes away the blood, the crimson drops mixing with the water in a beautiful dance of finality, I make a plan for disposal.

Tonight, I lost my last piece of solace, of peace, of happiness. If that's not bad enough, I lost my repairman, my best friend-my *only* friend. Add the overwhelming humiliation of him and his friends knowing and seeing me so vulnerable, so freaking broken...

I shake my head as tears mix with the now-clean water. And just like the blood, there's nothing left. I have no family, no friends, and no way to have any safe "social calls."

It's all tainted. All dirty. All so durn screwed up.

Shutting the water off, I get to work, cleaning up a mess of my own making, and desperately wish the universe would give me a freaking break for once.

~CHAPTER 20~

Beatrice

Two Weeks Later

Nightmares have rocked my world every single night. My shoulder and cuts are now healed, and most of the bruising from that night has faded. All that's really left is a gnarly scar from where that jerkface bit me and some tenderness in my ribs.

It only took me a couple of hours to dispose of my guests. It's not my favorite thing, which is why I usually asked Stu. It took me way too long, but I was working against cracked ribs, and my shoulder screamed in agony every time I moved it.

Afterward, I scrubbed my skin raw, cried until I lost my voice and all my tears dried up, then promptly fell into bed.

As I drain my, like, seventh Diet Coke of the day, I find myself relieved that I'm almost finished with the last class of the week. My phone notifies me of an app message, but I ignore it while I review the homework for the day and remind them that our unit test is next week.

Once my students log out, I stare long and hard at my computer. Memories of all the sordid, jacked-up stuff I've been through play through my mind like a horror film.

Dad abandoning me.

Mom marrying an abusive drunk.

My step-cousins harassing me every chance they got.

Years of bullying and harassment from peers and my stepdad about my weight.

My so-called best friend manipulating me into having sex; no warm-up, no fondling, no kissing... Just ripping my vagina open with a nine-and-a-half-inch dick without lube. Pumping four times before cumming, then driving us to school in silence.

Him ignoring me after... then spreading rumors about me begging him to sleep with me, rumors about me stalking him, and, of course, rumors that I was the worst lay ever.

Becoming a social pariah, even more than I already was.

Mom kicking me out of the house at 18 in favor of her shitty husband who loved calling me a cunt and a whore.

Working two full-time jobs to pay for my own school, plus trying to pay rent.

Being backed into the corner of the burger shack I worked at by my boss. (Who was also my friend's Dad's best friend).

Him taunting me with the few tips and leftovers I desperately needed in order to pay the electric bill and afford some boxed macaroni.

His big, meaty hand, stuffing the money down the front of my pants as his vodka-steeped breath burned my skin.

The bald man from the bar who followed me home, pushed his way into my apartment, and took every orifice I had.

Blood

Tears

So many dang tears.

My vision tunnels and I begin to feel woozy, which, helpfully, causes me to blink out of the past before the last 8 years could surface. Lord knows things only got worse.

Blinking out of the pathetic playback of my life, I snatch my phone off the table next to me and make my way into the kitchen. I open the pantry, then the fridge, then the freezer... and then amble back to the pantry. I've barely eaten since that night. I know I can't live off of Diet Coke and the occasional trail mix bar, but right now, I just don't have it in me to care.

I. Don't. Care.

There are no more smiles, no more tears, no more anything. I can't even get into a book. And reading is life- or, it was.

Now, well...

A ding on my phone distracts me momentarily, and I heave a painful sigh. Swiping the screen open, I find two new messages in my kink finder app. After a brief internal debate, I meander through the living room and fall ungracefully across my couch. For at least twenty seconds, I stare up at my phone, now hovering over my face.

Deciding to just get it over with, I click the app open to see that E has messaged me. He's messaged a couple of times since we met, but I've only sent surface-level responses. Home-boy must be desperate to be still trying. But, still, it's...*nice.*

Alpha has also messaged me a few times, but I always make excuses not to be able to meet. I haven't felt the least bit attractive and definitely didn't need him asking questions about my cuts and bruises.

Then, there's Stu. He calls and sends messages almost daily. But I haven't responded to a single one. He brought people into my home- *men* into my home. Yes, they saved me. But, then, he also showed them something that could absolutely land me in jail. Honestly, I'm still waiting for the police or FBI to knock my door down.

Almost dropping my phone on my face, I quickly remember that I was about to read messages from E. Pushing aside Stu's betrayal, I click on the message icon and imagine my big COD soldier.

> **E:** I'm so bored at work! Wanna play a game?

> **E:** Promise it won't hurt. <wink emoji>

A ghost of a smile graces my lips for the first time in the last couple of weeks. I almost ask him what he does for work, but then I remember the rules. *My* rules.

Snuggling further into the couch, I respond.

> **Me:** Sure. But, sometimes pain reminds us we're alive.

> **E:** Ha! Too true baby girl.

> **E:** Ok, Twenty Questions...

> **Me:** No! Lol

> **E:** I'll tell you what, we play 5 questions, and I'll return the favor. But, be warned, if I have to narrow down my questions, there won't be a lot of "easy" ones.

I tug my lip into my mouth, my teeth almost piercing through. The man has a way with words. And his body... hot dang!

Me: Ok, fine. <eyeroll emoji> But, you have to answer your own questions, too.

E: You got it baby girl.

E: I'll start easy with you. Because I'm a gentleman.

I giggle out and shake my head. *Gentleman my butt.*

E: What's your favorite food?

Me: Not easy! I'm a fattie and love food. Orange chicken, puffy tacos, Green Goddess Salad from Panera, and I'm an absolute slut for a good cheesesteak. No cheese sauce though. That ain't right.

E: Young lady... if you were here I'd redden that ass. Don't ever refer to yourself as fat again. You're sexy, curvy, soft, and a-fucking-mazing.

Me: <eyeroll emoji> I've already let you screw me. You don't have to flatter me.

E: I'm officially counting your punishments. That's 2.

I scoff aloud and roll my eyes heavenward. He's laying it on a little thick but, what the heck, it doesn't hurt to pretend.

E: Ok, ok... I'm a foodie too but I could absolutely eat bacon cheeseburgers daily. Sides must be switched up but a good, juicy burger is heaven.

Me: You like juicy meat. Got it. <wink emoji>

E: In fact, I very much do. But that's another conversation. Next question: Happiest memory?

I'm still thinking about what he meant by his previous statement. I don't remember seeing on his profile that he was bi or anything.

My face flushes with heat as I imagine him kissing another man. A familiar tingle begins to make its way through my body and I shiver involuntarily. Wetness pools in my panties and I have to forcefully shake myself out of my lusty daze.

Re-reading the second question, tears form in my eyes. I don't have a lot of those, to be honest. Zig-zagging my way through my past, I try to find happy moments. Birthdays sucked, and friends were few and far between. Landing my first teaching job was great, but it wasn't what I considered "happy." Just... relieved I could possibly help others the way no one helped me. It also didn't hurt that I did something more with my life than my stepdad ever said I would.

Images of Stu cross through my mind. The first night we met, I was in the middle of doling out a little justice. His lazy grin and bright blue eyes caught me off guard. His hair was messy in that "I don't care" kind of way that is insanely sexy. His piercings were at complete odds with his playful, golden retriever vibe. My silly, sweet Stu.

I feel the scowl on my face deepen as I reprimand myself. *Not mine. Never mine.*

> **Me:** Meeting my best friend... now ex-friend. He was always such a bright spot in my dark world. You?
>
> **E:** Why aren't you friends anymore? I can't imagine you in a dark world. You are the light. Trust me. <Wink emoji>
>
> **Me:** He betrayed me. He wasn't the first, but he will be the last. Ok, too personal. Next?
>
> **E:** Ok, baby girl. But, I'm here if you need to vent or talk.

We spent the next ten minutes messaging back and forth. His questions veered off from general questions to more sexy questions, which I was wonderfully thankful for...until I wasn't.

I got so wrapped up in our little nonsense bubble and divulged one of my biggest fantasies: more than one man at a time. I'm pretty sure I made him uncomfortable when I added that if any of the guys also play together, it would make it hotter.

After three minutes of him not responding, I told him I had a meeting and closed the app.

Too much. I'm always too much.

~CHAPTER 21~

Even

I've spent the better part of the last 4 hours consumed by thoughts of Bea and the little bit of herself she shared with me. Right after I sent her the last question, Charlie showed up, dragging in his bags and tactical gear; his favorite guitar bag slung across his shoulder.

It took us a bit to get him settled back in, and then I made dinner; momentarily forgetting that I never saw if Bea answered my final question. The guys and I sat around the table; eating in uncomfortable silence.

After leaving Bea's two weeks ago, the drive home was stupidly silent. Charlie vibrated with barely concealed tension, and the others were just as high-strung.

Once we walked into the house, though, Charlie exploded. He revealed that he had been meeting with her through some video streaming service a few times a month. He didn't realize it was her until he entered her bedroom and saw the vinyl records displayed on her wall. Something about Prince that I didn't fully understand. Apparently, she wore a mask when they were together each time, and he had his face concealed in darkness. But, when she rounded the corner, he saw the flower tattoo on her arm and officially knew.

And that sent Stu into a whole other spiral. He *just* came out for an actual meal two nights ago. He plopped on the couch next to Danny and me, silently picked up a controller, and joined us in playing COD for almost three hours while munching on some pizza.

Charlie had been missing in action since the day after everything happened at Beatrice's. Danny and I drove him back to La Porte to pick up his bike; he mumbled something about tying up loose ends and rode away without a backward glance.

When he showed up tonight, he didn't even tell us anything. Just walked in with his stuff, unloaded, ate dinner, and locked himself in his room.

Now, Danny and I are alone and snuggled up in bed. I take out my phone to share what I learned and to let him know she's doing well. I know he's been silently pining after the strong, gentle, yet scared woman he met just a few weeks ago. All of his protector instincts have kicked in, and he's been slightly more brash with me than usual. But I get it. I've been a little distracted, too.

Reading our messages aloud, I feel Danny relax fully into the bed. That is, until we read the response to her biggest fantasy. Danny's whole body lights up like a Christmas tree and a hopeful gleam sparks in his eyes.

I still haven't responded to Bea; not yet. I know she's probably been overthinking my lack of response since she sent it, but I need to think about what to do next. I also need to have a conversation with Danny and the others before making a decision.

I texted the guys around 9 this morning, asking them to meet me in the living room. The others made their way here in about ten minutes. But we're still waiting for Charlie.

Stu's leaning against the bar cart in the corner. Heavy, black bags sag underneath his eyes, and his hair appears flatter, greasier than normal. I can only assume he hasn't heard from Beatrice since she kicked us out. My heart aches for him, but Danny and I have a plan. Well, the makings of one. And, if we're going to pull this off, we need to do it together.

Charlie ambles in with his hair tousled from sleep and a pair of low-hanging navy sweatpants and seemingly falls onto the couch. For the first time, maybe ever, Stu doesn't try to sneak a look or make a humorous comment about his trouser snake. Instead, he stands still, his breathing barely perceptible, as appears to become one with the bar cart.

Clearing my throat, I stand in the middle of the room, garnering the attention of my best friends; my family.

As I share the "rough draft" version of what Danny and I came up with, I watch Charlie and Stu for their tells. Stu's whole body has become tense, his slim, lean muscles rippling with barely contained anger and lust. Conversely, Charlie is completely relaxed, leaning against the couch with his legs spread and his arms resting on the back of the couch. However, the tenting of his sweatpants tells me he's *very* interested.

After a tense silence, Stu's resolve snaps. "Are you out of your fucking mind!" He's across the room, standing in front of me, with four strides of his long legs. Spittle hits my face as his rage boils over. "You want to trick her? She kicked me out, kicked us out. She doesn't know who you actually are! You think me letting you see her little dungeon and letting you into her home hurt her? Do you have any idea what this could do to her?"

As he finishes his rant, he turns and paces, pulling his fingers tightly through his scalp and letting out a sound that is pure agony. I can almost hear the tears filling his eyes, and he truly shows us for the first time in days, just how much losing Bea's friendship broke him.

Stepping forward, I grasp his shoulder and quietly assure him, "I get it. I do. But, she *wants* this. In fact, I know she wants you, me, and Charlie...and I know she would love Danny. But her walls, man..." I shake my head as I think about the fortress this amazing woman has built around her. "She needs help breaking down those walls. And we're the ones to do it. She craves dominance in the bedroom but wraps it *tightly* in BDSM practices. That way, she's still in control."

Swallowing the lump in my throat, I pat his back softly, letting my words sink in. Then, I step back and address the room: "She's already told me that it's her greatest fantasy. And, if we can give that to her, I know it will work out—for all of us."

With a final look around the room, I nod my head and retreat to the gym. I know this could work. And, technically, it's not lying if she agrees to it.

But first, I need *them* to agree; then I can work on her.

~CHAPTER 22~

Beatrice

A little over a week has now passed since I heard from E. And it's been three weeks since I last saw Stu, since the last time I tried to be intimate, since the last time I was sort of happy. And every single day feels like darkness crowds my heart and shadows my soul.

And, frankly, I'm done.

Tonight, I stayed logged on much longer than usual so I could complete two weeks of lesson plans and get every assignment my students have done updated in the gradebook. Then, I sent a letter of resignation to my boss. I wiped the laptop drive, boxed it up, and put a return label on it. I'll drop it off with the letter I wrote to Stu at the post office in the morning.

Now, I'm working on my own laptop. I update my will, leaving everything to Stu. I may hate him right now, but I know from the few times we traded personal details that he didn't have a great upbringing. And, honestly, I don't know anyone else; *lucky him.*

Sending off the final pieces to my lawyer, I wipe this laptop and tuck it away on my bookshelf. Clicking my phone open, I pair it to my speaker and click on my 'Just Let Me Be in My Feelings' playlist. Vampire by Olivia Rodrigo begins to play through the room and my heart lurches for the first time in days. Ignoring the familiar tingle of pain, I set my phone down and head out of the living room.

Ready to do some deep cleaning, I stride into the kitchen and begin clearing out the meager contents. I haven't been very hungry so there's not much to go through. I pluck the cardboard box I had saved in the garage and begin filling it with non-perishable items to donate tomorrow. Everything else gets tossed.

As the song reaches its crescendo, I feel the burn of tears accumulating in my eyes. My throat clogs with emotions trying to make their way out, but I quickly shut that crap down.

I make quick work of spraying down the shelves and cleaning them; followed by all the little nooks and crannies. Then, I start on the freezer. After trashing all of the contents and wiping down the interior, I briefly debate throwing out the Mint Chocolate Chip ice cream. Deciding to finish it later, I put it back in the freezer, with a confirming nod, and shut the door. Then, I give the pantry the same treatment; putting anything non-perishable in the donation box and tossing everything else out.

I'm a little sweaty and irritated that I'm nowhere near finished. Looking down, I notice the trash bag is overflowing and bulging on every side. Mumbling under my breath, I tie it up, heft it out, and toss it in the large trash bin outside.

When I re-enter the house, my phone pings with a notification. Which, conveniently, reminds me that I need to wipe my phone tomorrow, too.

Grabbing the final book in the series I've been reading, and my phone, I ditch the cleaning effort and decide to use my last bath bomb. *Might as well, right? Besides, I need to find out if Annie gets her happily ever after.*

Five minutes later, I'm chest-deep in a scalding lavender soak. It's sheer perfection. I can hear the music wafting through the living room, into my bedroom, and quietly filtering into the bathroom. Steam fills the air and mingles with the lyrics of Tired by Labrinth and Zendaya. The song melds perfectly with my soul and I realize just how much I currently identify with it.

Another notification pings on my phone, bringing me out of my silent reverie. Swiping the screen, I see that E has contacted me in the app. I worry my lip between my teeth as I hesitate to open it. We had such a great conversation, and then, poof, he was gone. It didn't hurt. It shouldn't hurt. But it stung. A little.

Remembering my plan for Sunday night, I choose to respond to him. I should at least tell him...something. Just to make sure he doesn't try to reach out again.

> **E:** Sorry about last week. My roommate came home and needed help unpacking. Then work got crazy and... yeah. I'm so sorry.

> **E:** Anyways, I was reaching out to see what you thought about making your fantasy come true?

I feel myself frown in confusion. *What the heck is he talking about?*

E: So, I don't know if I told you this before, but I have a boyfriend. We've actually shared women before, and our two best friends have frequently joined us.

E: Not the other guys with my boyfriend and me, but the four of us with a woman.

E: I know that may sound strange or whatever but it works for us. Well, I mean, it has the few times we've tried it in the past.

E: Anyways, I can't stop thinking about you and I'd really like to give you everything.

E: Not everything, everything but, you know. This one thing. Then, who knows. But, at least you can cross it off your bucket list. <wink emoji>

A giggle escapes me. He's usually so confident but he's clearly getting flustered. It's kind of cute. *What the heck? No, no, no. Stop it. Remember the plan.*

I chew my lip momentarily as the warm, heavenly bath works its magic on my body. Images of our last encounter move through my mind and goosebumps scatter across my flesh.

One more meeting couldn't hurt. One more fling. One more time to maybe feel something. And, living out my fantasy may be the perfect way to end the weekend.

Before, I end it all.

~CHAPTER 23~

Beatrice

Last night, I agreed to this stupid idea—but only after spending an hour researching the place he wanted to meet. Somehow, E knew there was no way I'd meet at their place, which he shares with these three other men. But he also didn't bother asking if they could come here. Instead, he invited me to be his guest at The Raven Room.

After one phone call, four emails with the manager reading policies and contracts, and sending the updated medical information I got from my appointment last week, I finally gave in. I sent a list of requirements for him and his friends to agree to, then, we set a date.

Now, in approximately three hours, I'll be walking into The Raven Room. Tonight is their annual Halloween party, which is perfect for me. The guys and I will blend in with everyone else dressing up, and we'll all be in masks. I let E know what my mask would look like, and he gave me strict orders not to wear panties.

I took care of everything I needed to do today. All trash has been emptied, food has been donated, and my work computer and Stu's letter have been sent.

Now, I'm spending some time soaking in the bath. Blue October's agonizingly pain-filled lyrics in Hate Me fester deep in my soul, and I find myself breaking down with each new bar.

A sob breaks from my chest, and every emotion in the universe spills down my cheeks, swirling with the water below.

I cry for the family I lost, for the family I never had.

I cry, knowing that the little girl I once was should have been better, should have *had* better.

I cry for the people I thought I could count on, the people who let me down.

I cry for the ones who dared take what wasn't theirs.

I cry, and I cry, and I cry.

The well inside of me fissures, and pain courses through my body as my emotions boil over.

They're too big, too painful.

I swipe my razor off the side of the tub and repeatedly slice it across my right hip. The sting forces my body to jump, but I ignore it and continue slashing the razor over the area of tender flesh. I feel myself begin to shake as little ribbons of crimson dance through the bath in a tantalizing motion.

A few beats pass until my body trembles with adrenaline, and my tears finally subside. Thankfully, the pain has now moved from my heart to my hip; effectively transferring into a more manageable area.

Feeling like a weight has lifted off my chest, I suck in a deep breath before slowly standing from the bath. Blood trails down my leg. Not heavy and thick, but thin and light; like a steady stream meandering through the woods.

Stepping out of the bath, I immediately move into the shower to actually clean my body and hair. As a shaky breath squeaks past my lips, a small grin tugs at my face. The lingering sting of the shallow cuts on my hip continues to ground me and keep me moving forward.

The song changes, pairing perfectly with my relieved mood as You Don't Own Me by Saygrace plays through the speaker.

I don't give a flying squirrel sack what anyone says about cutting. I prefer tattoos, yes, but sometimes you need to be grounded quickly, and thin, quick, shallow slits across fleshy spots do that trick every time. I'm not trying to kill myself- well, not tonight anyway- but it definitely helps when emotions become too much. A little trick I learned long ago after Matt's betrayal hurt as much as actually losing my virginity.

Once I'm finished and dried off, I get to work massaging my legs and arms. Johnson's Baby Oil with Shea and Cocoa Butter is one of the few moisturizers that doesn't break me out and leaves my skin impossibly smooth.

Excited energy buzzes under my skin as I finish preparing for my last night on Earth. Although I'm horrifically nervous the other three men won't find me good enough to play with, I'm choosing to trust E; as he assured me they will. Besides, worst comes to worst, E and I have already played, so I'll still have one man to spend the evening with.

It will take me an hour to get there, so I quickly rummage through my closet and pull things off the hangers. I throw on the black, ripped skinny jeans that accentuate the curves of my legs and rear, which E claims to like so much. The scratching pressure against the cuts on my hips helps to keep me in the moment and I quickly find a top to throw on. I'm not cute, I'm not sexy, so I'm not bothering to be anything other than me.

If they don't like it, I'll just get drunk and maybe speed up my little plan.

My lace blue bra from ThirdLove matches the delicately laced blue mask I'm wearing tonight. Wanting to show it off a little, along with my three black bird tattoos that sits on my collarbone, I opt for a black off-shoulder top that bunches just enough around my waist that it hides my hideous belly.

Now, the shoes. I tossed my dang Chucks, unable to look at them again after my last failed tryst, so now I'm stuck between peep-toe, black lace-up sandals, simple black flats, or knee-length black boots with black glittery laces that criss-cross in the back. They do zip, of course, so I won't have to worry about fumbling around when taking my shoes off. But that still doesn't really feel like me, so I opt for the simple, black flats.

I straighten my hair and give my side-swept bangs a little lift before putting on my makeup. I'm a simple girl, so nothing major. No contouring or shading. Just foundation, eyeliner, mascara, a dabble of light gray-to-white eyeshadow, and some blush. Of course, I add a little Dreamer Matte Ink and call it a day—or night, I suppose.

Grabbing my mask, I head out to the garage and pause for a moment. Yes, I did my hair but... if this is my last night, shouldn't I do it *my* way?

With a confident smirk, I grab my small, black backpack, slide off my flats and stuff them inside along with my mask, change my shoes, and head back out. Regardless of the men I'm meeting, I'm definitely going to make sure tonight's good.

~CHAPTER 24~

Charlie

Even's plan is dangerous at best. But what can I say? We all like a little danger.

When we originally met in La Porte, we were all hell-bent on tracking those assholes down. I was so excited when Stu said we found them. But, that excitement quickly morphed into intense determination when he said they were meeting their next victim.

I took off for the truck, not even bothering with my bike, and didn't look back until I was in the driver's seat and starting the truck. Once I saw that Stu had turned a ghostly shade of pale while searching for the victim's information, I immediately sensed that he had some kind of relationship with the woman that the vile bastard had been messaging. Then, hearing Danny scream out, the one who is usually either silent and deadly or sweet and bouncy- yeah, I knew she had to be amazing for them to show so much emotion.

However, nothing could have prepared me for the instantaneous surge of protectiveness I felt when I saw her lying still on the ground while that asshole pawed at her. It was dark, but the sky was clear so I saw enough.

Until I saw red.

I almost pulled her away from Stu but my brain registered the raw horror that took over his face. She *really* meant something to him.

Don't get me wrong, I was all too happy to help Danny wrestle the asshole to the ground before stomping on his head. His beast was far too close to the surface and I was already wondering how we would get him out. Thankfully, he was able to pull back, but I'm pretty sure it was because he knew Beatrice needed help.

Then, the surprises kept coming. Her house being so close was *definitely* not a coincidence, and piecing together the little details I've learned about her, I'm pretty sure *she* chose it. She likes to be in control, and based on her reaction to us being in her house last week, she's had that control taken away too many times.

The dungeon, on the other hand, was a surprise I *never* saw coming. Stu still won't talk much about it but assures me she "does what she needs to do to keep others safe." The entire statement was loaded with unspoken trauma. For now, I won't push.

But the cherry on the proverbial shitstorm of a sundae was finding out *she* was Omega. My Omega! What kind of small-ass town are we living in where that's even possible?

The second Even and I walked through her bedroom, I froze. It felt like a whole ice bucket of water was dumped straight on my head as I saw the entire left side of her bedroom wall decorated in vinyl records; that dang Purple Rain one mounted just to the side, where I had seen it before, through the laptop camera, as my cock was standing at full mast for her.

And just in case I wasn't totally sure it was *her*, that little, sassy spitfire walked into the living room, and I noticed the large tattoo on her forearm with the lily sitting front and center. I hadn't seen it before our last night on camera. But she was always skittish when I brought up personal stuff, so I didn't ask.

I can't lie, she was even more glorious, more stunning in person. Even bruised and cut up, she had this presence about her. Her blue, soulful eyes were filled with equal parts trauma and grit; of brokenness and sheer determination. My hands have been on my dick more in the last couple of weeks than it has in the last two months. I should be worried about chafing but I just can't help it.

Clearly, I'm not the only one fucked up over this woman as we're all piled in my truck on our way to meet her at our favorite club. And, honestly, I can't figure out how I feel. This woman is an enigma in her own right, and I can't lie; I'm more curious to see how this goes than I've let on.

I shift in my seat as my cock hardens painfully. I shouldn't feel so much about this woman already. Sure, we've met quite a few times in our video room, but I was literally in her actual presence for less than 10 minutes, and I already feel an inexplicable need to see her, love her, fucking hold her. How am I supposed to do that when I can't tolerate touch? I barely tolerate the guys patting me on the back.

My ex's death fucked me in more ways than ten. Over the last couple of years, I've learned that *I* can touch, because I can control it, but that's it. That's the line. Other people touching me makes me lose myself completely, and it's never pretty.

I take a few deep breaths, my hands clenching into fists as I try to regain my composure. Thinking of Cammy always throws me off and I can't afford to be off tonight.

We pull into The Raven Room's parking lot and jump out of my truck. Slipping on our masks, we take in each other's costumes for the night.

Even is in his favorite COD mask and gear. Obviously, he doesn't have the ammo, knives, or helmet. He does have on his black tac vest and black cargo pants. He also fashions a set of headphones with a mic over his head. He's hoping she won't recognize him with just the bottom part of his face covered since he only met her a couple of times without his gear.

Next to him, Stu is wearing a Ghostface mask, a fitted black V-neck shirt, and black jeans. Strangely, he paired them with red Chucks, but it kind of works. He needed a full mask since his piercings would absolutely give him away—that, and probably his voice.

Danny's bouncing up and down on the balls of his feet like a sugar-fueled kangaroo. The loon has a full skull mask on. The top is of a white skull with creepy ass cracks through it. The skull part stops after the top row of teeth before turning into long, white lines trailing down the rest of the black mask. It heavily resembles The Punisher, which fits him perfectly. He has on a fitted, black, long-sleeved shirt to cover the tats on his arms, just in case Bea recognizes them since they all hung out one night... since she saw him the night of the attack. He also has black gloves with skeleton fingers bubbled on top and khaki cargo pants.

Then, there's me. I don't really do the whole "masked thing," but for Bea, I'm willing to give it a try. I channeled my inner horror lover and bought a red Jason mask that's striped with black paint for an additional creep factor. Not knowing what else to wear with it, I chose a black, sleeveless button-up shirt—with the first few buttons undone, of course. Then, I paired it with my combat boots and black jeans.

The four of us look like complete psychopaths, but judging by the looks we're getting from the women going inside, I guess that's not a bad thing.

I look at my watch and see that it's just about 9:30, so I tilt my chin in the direction of the club. Just as we step forward to cross the lot, the purring of a motorcycle brings us to a halt. There are a few in the lot, but most people won't ride a motorcycle to a club because, well, safety.

I can tell I'm not the only one intrigued by the sound as the others have paused and turned towards the road. We watch someone drive into the lot on a Phantom Purple Yamaha R3. The lights around the parking lot glint off the purple and you can see the faint strokes of the pink lines that ombre down the sides. The motorcycle turns down our aisle, making its way past us. The parking lot lights are just bright enough that I can see the rider's gray Dainese shoes; the familiar devil symbol in purple stitched on the side.

Danny steps up next to me and tilts his head, making him truly look like the psychopath he actually is with The Punisher mask on. Stu and Even come to a stand next to us, and we watch with rapt attention as the person parks, turns off the bike, and stands, straddling the bike almost on tip-toes.

I was pretty sure before, but now I'm 100% positive that the rider is a woman. Her ass looks downright biteable in her skinny jeans. Her shirt hangs off of one shoulder and I can see the faint lining of a blue lace bra. My dick is already way too happy as my eyes slowly peruse this voluptuous creature.

Shucking off her gloves, she moves to dismount and then removes the little black backpack on her back. It takes her a moment to remove her shoes and trade them for a pair of black flats. Her breasts bounce with the movements as she's bent over; that juicy ass high in the air.

Standing taller, she begins to move the helmet. The lights refract off the iridescent swirls decorating the black helmet, giving it a magical yet badass look.

She then ducks down between the bike and the truck next to her, slides off her helmet, and shakes out her hair. *And fuck my life; it's her!* Her back is facing us, and she's bent over to hide her face, but I know with every pulse of my dick that the woman who just rode up on a damn motorcycle is Beatrice.

Judging by the gasps and grunts around me, I'm not the only one who didn't know this woman drove a motorcycle. Looking over at Stu, he shrugs and shakes his head, "I never peeked under the covers in the garage. But, now I need to know what's under the others."

His voice is heavily distorted behind the mask, making me chuckle. Even shakes his head and goes back to watching Bea. She slips her riding shoes back into her bag and brushes her shoulder-length hair out before fixing the mask to her face. "Let's get inside before she sees us. I don't want her to run if she thinks we saw her without a mask."

With a nod, we turn and quickly move to the club door. My dick is already trying to punch its way through my pants, and we haven't even talked to her yet. This is either going to be the best night ever or the worst. There's no doubt in my mind that there won't be any in-between.

~CHAPTER 25~

Beatrice

My little mask is clipped to the sides of my hair. It's half silver and half light blue, and it matches my bra color perfectly. Instead of a whole mask, I went for one that covers most of my forehead, down to my nose. It flares out on both sides, reminding me of an old Victorian masquerade mask. The mask's left half is a shimmery silver with wispy blue lines randomly decorating it. The right side is blue, but instead of silver lines decorating it, there's a 3D silver butterfly wing that spans past the top and bottom of the mask. It's delicate and beautiful and makes me feel pretty. And, tonight, I deserve to feel pretty.

Walking into The Raven Room, the host, who introduces himself as William, searches for my name on his tablet. I can't help but smile as he is, honest to God, wearing red sequin bottoms and a tuxedo vest. His wrists are adorned with what appears to be white cuffs. It looks like he cut them off of a white dress shirt and wore them as bracelets. His whole body is riding that edge of skinny and lean muscle and his smile is absolutely infectious.

After finding my name, he asks for my ID and shows me to my assigned locker. After showing me how to set the code, I throw in my bag, keys, and helmet before turning towards him.

While William checks in the next patron, I take in the very dark, very black, very plain front room. The steady thumping of a bass beats through the walls. A few red and white lights are scattered around the perfectly square room. The lights beam from the bottom up, casting a sensual, mysterious glow.

On the far wall, there's a long, rectangular desk with a computer and a fierce-looking woman typing away on it. I assume she's the one I spoke to on the phone. She's not dressed anywhere near how William is dressed, though. Granted, the desk is blocking her lower half, but her top half boasts of a serious white blouse and a no-nonsense ponytail combed to perfection. She's talking in low tones with a huge brickhouse of a man and they appear to be going over paperwork.

William clamors excitedly about it being my first time and how I'm just going to *love* everything and everyone. We easily banter back and forth about all they offer, and he *gushes* about how hot a group of masked men that just walked through were.

After a few minutes, I'm finished signing the documents I was required to do in person, and I suddenly feel sad that I'm leaving him here. I guess he can sense that I was momentarily sulking because he bumps me with his hip, tells me he gets off at 1:00 am, and wants to have a drink as I "spill all the juicy gossip from the night."

Then, with a wink and a nudge, he shoos me through the door—the one black door.

Entering the club is like stepping into one of my steamy romance novels. Closer by Nine Inch Nails bumps through the speakers, and the sound waves seem to directly affect the thrumming, gyrating bodies spread around the club. Similar to the lobby, the main source of lighting comes from red lights strategically placed around the walls near the floor. However, the only white lights found in the room are dim, and positioned over the four golden cages with people dancing in them. The difference in the lighting causes them to stand out, but the dullness of the single, white lights casts the entertainers in an erotic glow.

Additionally, there are black leather booths lined up along the three far walls. Some of them face toward the wall, which I find odd, while many face toward the center of the club. Anywhere between 3 and 7 people occupy most of the booths already, and the patrons appear to be all too open about making out publicly.

Everyone seems to have really embraced the Halloween theme and are dressed one of two ways: basically not at all, or in some kind of actual costume. Fairies, Vikings, Roman leaders, sexy nurses, horror villains—you name it, someone is probably wearing it—or wearing some of it.

The large space probably fits about 200 people comfortably. On the wall directly to my right is a long bar with shelves on shelves of every liquor known to man. A woman who can't be older than 25 flits back and forth taking orders with her very best customer service smile. She must be used to people giving orders to her boobs because she doesn't bat an eye. Then again, she's walking around with a red, leather mini-skirt and red, glittery pasty petals covering her nipples. The only other thing covering any part of her body are the black Vans she's wearing.

I slip closer to the bar as my nerves skyrocket. I haven't been to a club since the night I took out Baldie. A deep sense of dread threatens to consume me, but a bubbly voice breaks me free of its hold. "What can I getcha hot stuff?"

I look towards the bartender, then around me wondering who she's referring to. She leans over with a playful eye roll, "Yes, I'm talking to you. I effing LOVE the mask! How did you find one to match your bra?" She asks conversationally.

It takes me a moment to remember how to be normal, but thankfully, my brain eventually catches up. "I have a whole bin of masks. Every time I come across one I like, I buy it. This one just so happened to match my bra, so I went with it." I giggle at how ridiculous it sounds, then order a Tequila Sunrise and a shot of Patron Silver. I need all the liquid courage tonight. And, it's my last night so I might as well milk it for all it's worth.

With a bright smile, she gets to work on both of my drinks, and, before I know it, she's sliding them my way. I pay with cash and leave extra for tip.

"Name's Ama. I know most of the regulars here so I could kind of tell you were new. This place really is all it claims to be."

She points to a few men discreetly placed around the room. "Security is very particular and they're more of 'toss them out, then ask questions' kind of guys. But I've worked here for two years, and only four people have ever been tossed out; memberships canceled. They're *all* about creating a safe, fun, consensual environment. If you need anything, don't hesitate to ask." Her smile is blinding and she seems completely genuine. I can't help but mirror it with my own as I thank her and slip out of the way for the next person to order.

I slam my shot, slide the glass to the back of the bar so no one bumps it, and begin to wander around the room.

The entire atmosphere is primal, intoxicating, and so dang aphrodisiacal. I make my way through the throng of people dancing, kissing, and- *oh, my, is she giving that guy a blowjob on the floor? Holy fork! How does she hold her breath for that long?*

Seeming to hear my inner thoughts, the woman wearing a sexy nurse outfit, or parts of it, locks eyes with me and I can see her mouth widen with a smile. She enjoys being watched. *Wow. I wish I had that confidence.*

With a smile and a friendly nod, I make my way to the other side of the room where four golden cages are displayed. Behind them is a small, rounded corner bar, and I am momentarily distracted by a mountainous man throwing bottles and shaking drinks like he used to be in a circus.

Sipping on my drink, I return my focus to the people in the cages. Marilyn Manson's Tainted Love blares through the speakers, and the lights above the cages blink along with the music.

In one cage is a tall, leggy woman with midnight black hair. She sways her hips to the rhythm in a sexy, almost freeing dance. Her hands slide against her toned body, already dripping with sweat, as she closes her eyes and appears to get lost in the feeling of her body.

The couple in the second cage is clothed in devilish outfits that appear to be made out of leather. He's gripping her throat and dominating her mouth as he slides his fingers in and out of her pussy. They are completely lost in each other as they grind and sway to the beat.

A slurping sound rings out around me, and I realize that I'm sucking the air at the end of my drink. A little bit of embarrassment sparks through me before I realize that no one in this dang room is paying attention to boring, 'ol me.

Realizing I'm still alone in the club, I briefly wonder if I've been stood up.

Deciding to make the best of it, I head to the corner bar and order another shot and drink. With a quick flick of my head, the delightful burn of tequila works its way through my system. I hum in satisfaction as I literally feel each of my muscles begin to relax.

Taking my fresh drink, I head back to the cages and watch as a woman squats close to the front bars, legs spread wide as she allows the other club-goers to touch and tease her. The whole ordeal is incredibly risqué and must be so freeing. I've never considered myself a voyeur, but I'm definitely more than a little turned on.

As the song ends, a man's energetic voice filters through the room. "Welcome to The Raven Room my little deviants. I hope you all *enjoy* yourselves tonight. While you do, don't forget it's our very own, Ama's, birthday!" A round of cheers and applause threatens to deafen me as we all turn toward the mostly naked bartender. She's shaking her tits and smiling widely.

"Now, she's still on the clock, but she *gets off...*" His voice trails off after his second innuendo. An insane amount of catcalls and wolf whistles swirl with the shouts roaring through the crowd. I can just imagine he's smirking and I chuckle to myself. *They must be friends.*

"Alright, you animals, she gets *off* at 10:30, so buy her all the drinks and make sure she has fun!" With another loud cheer from the crowd, the mic cuts and the music begins. Jeremih's Birthday Sex begins to play and I smile at, yet another obvious innuendo.

Wanting to make her birthday special, since she was so sweet to me, I make my way back over to her side of the bar. She spots me and waves enthusiastically. After serving a few more people, she prances over. I ask her for another shot, and she quickly fills the tiny glass. As soon as she places it down, I hand her $100 and giggle as her eyes light up with surprise. "Happy Birthday, Ama." I tell her with a smile.

She squeals and hugs me tightly before leaning back and wiping away a stray tear. "I just knew we'd be fast friends," she professes with a watery giggle. I can't help but smile back at her and wish I even knew what the word meant.

"Enjoy your birthday. I'll see ya later." I wave her back to the ever-growing line of thirsty clubgoers. She tinkles her fingers in a girly wave and turns to the next customer.

Throwing the tequila back, I set the empty glass back on the bar. My other drink is still firmly in hand as I turn on my heel and meander back towards the cages.

The music slithers through my body and mixes with the tequila. The heady buzz rushes through my veins, and I find myself closing my eyes while swaying my hips to the sensual music.

Not even a minute later, a large, warm hand touches my hip. I jump at the sudden intrusion before another hand clamps down on my other hip, effectively preventing me from turning. My heart rate doubles and fear has my vision tunneling.

Just as I'm about to spiral, a deep, growly voice cuts through the music. "Oh, dirty girl. Out here swaying that ass for just any ol' asshole to look at." As part of me relaxes into his embrace, recognizing the deep timber of his voice, another part of me coils tightly like a spring being compressed.

Warmth seeps into my back as he steps closer behind me, pressing his already hard cock into my back. He tilts my head with his, leaning in and inhaling deeply. His hands dig into my hips and he begins to grind and sway with me. A grin lifts my lips and I close my eyes, getting lost in the swaying and grinding of our bodies.

Unfortunately, the sudden realization that he may not be alone spikes my anxiety. Remembering the drink, that's now partially watered down, I suck down the rest of it greedily. The cooling sensation is the perfect partner to the warmth caused by the Tequila Sunrise.

I hadn't realized that I had stopped moving to suck down my drink until E chuckled in my hair. "Ok, baby girl, enough of that. How much have you had?"

His large hand leaves my hip and removes the cup from my hands. Stepping up next to me, he takes my hand and leads me towards the corner bar. One of his large steps is like two of mine, so I have to practically jog to catch up. But, while I do, I take a moment to check out his perfectly sculpted rear end. His pants hug every curve, and I happily follow those curves down his thick thighs.

Once he sets the cup on the bar, he turns around. I'm so busy ogling his backside that I don't quite catch the abrupt movement until I'm crashing into his chest. My hands come up to stop myself from face-planting. The tac vest, no longer filled with ammunition and knives, stretches across the broad expanse of his chest and stomach.

For a whole forking eternity, we stand there, breathing heavily as lust begins to bleed through my body. It's not until his hand cups my chin, tilting it upwards, that I realize I haven't even looked at him yet. Once our eyes meet, I notice that they aren't the color I thought they were. I thought his eyes were primarily brown and green, but with the additional lighting, they're actually a deep, dark blue and sea green. They are absolutely stunning.

I swallow heavily as E leans down; his soft mask brushing against my lips, sending little tingles down my spine. "How much have you had to drink?" His voice is low and almost menacing. I flush, feeling like I'm about to be reprimanded as I contemplate my answer. He puts me into subspace so effortlessly; it's insane.

"Um, two drinks. And, um, three shots."

I barely finish my answer before he follows up, "Of what?"

Blinking back the weird tears that are forming, I stutter out, "U-um, Tequila Sunrises and Tequila. That's it."

We stand there for a moment, my breaths coming in harsh pants, as his eyes flick between mine. "OK. Are you still up for this? I don't want you to-"

"Yes, please." My answer is a breathy plea. One that causes a spark to flicker in his eyes.

"OK, then. Let's go, baby girl." I can tell he's smirking because his face crinkles on one side. He interlaces our fingers together and leads me through the club towards a dark hallway I hadn't noticed.

"Ok, Sir," I reply shyly. My body trembles as butterflies form a mosh pit in my stomach. *Here we go...*

~CHAPTER 26~

Stu

Fucking, fuckity, fuck, fuck. We spent the last ten minutes staring at Beatrice, completely enraptured as she entered the club. The way her ass seemed to sway with the music no matter where she was in the room and how her eyes lit up as she watched the entertainers from behind her delicate mask had me hard as a rock.

I've loved her from afar for years, but tonight, I get to show her how good I can be for her, how good *we* can be. I trust these guys with my life, and after they stopped pushing for information about her, I realized I do trust them with *her,* too.

We've been visiting the place since it first opened seven years ago. The owner, Lola, opened this place to allow women to feel safe exploring their sexuality. Society's view on women's sexuality sucks. Lola hopes this place can help them explore those desires safely with like-minded people.

When Ama started, she became like a little sister to us. We know all of her tells, having watched over her so many times, and it was immediately apparent that she loved Beatrice from the moment they met.

After Jim, Lola's husband, announced Ama's birthday and began playing that song, I think we all lost our patience. We watched as Bea shuffled over to the bar and downed another shot. My knuckles turned white as she began sensually dancing by herself, her body swaying deliciously.

Even's control must have snapped as he abruptly stood and marched her way. The rest of us took that as our cue, the key to room 4 burning a hole in my pocket. We'd already decided he would approach her first, then bring her to us.

And now, here we are, pacing the room like animals in a cage.

Charlie grunts before he walks over to the speaker and clicks through the little phone secured to the cabinet. The Internet is connected, and the phone's BlueTooth is connected to a small speaker, but they were somehow able to disable all apps and messaging services, so the only working app is YouTube Music. This way, no pictures or videos could be leaked. Lola and Jim are very particular about privacy; something that helps all of the patrons feel comfortable.

Wicked Games by The Weeknd quietly drifts through the room. Danny busies himself lighting candles around the room, and I—well, I'm just trying to hide the fact that I'm trembling violently.

"You ok, Hacker?" Charlie's nickname for me rolls off his tongue. But, it's lacking its usual playfulness. I peer over at him and feel his all-knowing gaze bore into my mask. Even though he can't see my eyes, I know he can see my damn soul. *Perceptive bastard.*

With a shrug and a non-committal nod, I brush off his concern. I clear my throat, trying to dislodge the emotions that are threatening to drown me.

Two rapid knocks on the door make me jump right before it swings open.

Even's big bulky frame fills the doorway, and the air backs up in my lungs. With a barely perceptible nod, he steps into the room with Bea trailing behind him. I look down and notice she's gripping his hand so tightly that her knuckles are white.

The dim lighting in the room casts shadows across her face, but I can see her bright blue eyes across the room. She's a damn vision. Tight, black ripped jeans, a shirt hanging off her shoulder, showing off her little tattoo and her perfect fucking collarbone. I want to run to her and wrap her in a hug and beg her to forgive me...but I don't. I keep my feet glued to the floor.

Once she steps in, Even leans back behind her and locks the door with a *schnik*. As quiet as it is, it seems to echo throughout the room.

Bea leans back against the door, biting down on her perfect plump lip and spinning a little silver ring around her thumb. I've seen it before. It's an anxiety ring that rotates and says, "Just Breathe." I don't actually know if it helps her, but I do know she spins it constantly.

Even looks down at her, takes her hand in his, and asks, "Do you still want this, B? Want us all?"

Her eyes widen, and I see her body shiver. I stay perfectly still, barely breathing as she makes her decision.

She takes her time, taking us all in; separated around the room so as to not overwhelm her. After the longest moment of silence, she looks back at Even and nods.

"Words, baby girl." His voice deepens, signaling to the rest of us that his Dom is taking over.

Goosebumps scatter across her arms, and I watch as she squeezes her thighs together subtly. "Y-yes." It's barely above a whisper, but it's what Even needed, what we all needed.

It feels like a collective breath is released around the room, and we all shift as he whispers, "Good girl."

Stepping away from her, Even backs up towards the bed, never turning away from her. His voice is low and intense as he introduces each of us. Starting with Charlie, "I know you like the letter names, so we can stick with that." Going around the room, he nods at each of us, "This is C, that's D, and that's S."

Her whole body begins trembling, and I can see her eyes blown wide with lust already. It's taking every ounce of willpower I possess to stand here and wait for the signal.

With a lone finger, he summons her over. She takes a few tentative steps before standing in front of him. He gently moves his hands to her hips before positioning her to turn around with him, plastering his front to her back while facing out toward the rest of us.

"B is a very good girl," he purrs near her ear, causing her to shuffle a little. His hand travels from her hip, up over her shirt, to her breast. Then, he stops; he leaves it there like a silent command only she understands.

"But she really likes to be a dirty girl, don't you, baby girl?" Her eyes roll back, and she moans as her head falls against his shoulder.

He squeezes her breast roughly, her whimper causing my cock to throb painfully. "Y-yes, sir."

Groans echo around the room as we all step forward.

The guys move forward, but I hold my free hand up to stop them. "Before we get started, we need to be on the same page. I already let the guys know your preferences, but I want us all to be on the same page."

She nods shakily and whines as I move my hand back to her hip.

"You'll have to share, baby. This is your show. We're just here to pleasure you." She blushes the most beautiful crimson color, and I watch over her shoulder in fascination as it slowly travels down her neck. At the same time, I feel her body go rigid against mine, giving away how uncomfortable she is about vocalizing her needs. *We'll have to work on that.*

She bites her sexy lip and looks at the others standing around the room. I watch, enamored, as the flush spreads from her neck and across her chest. My dick is trying to unzip my pants for me, so I clench my fingers into her hips, trying to override the urge to strip her down and throw her on the bed right now.

She looks down at the ring she's been twirling since we walked in. Then, I watch as her shoulders beautifully roll back, her chin tilts up, and her whole body transforms into the goddamn queen I know she is.

"No kissing my mouth." She gives me a pointed look from the side of her eyes that's equal parts reprimand and lust. It makes sense now that I know her more. Kissing is too intimate for her. With a nod in agreement, I encourage her to continue.

"Lights off." She demands firmly.

Danny steps forward, tilting his head in a way that makes him look creepy as hell with that skull mask on. After two seconds, he counters, "Lights off, but candles lit."

His smooth voice is distorted perfectly behind the mask, and I find myself resisting the urge to squeeze my cock through my pants.

Beatrice wavers for a moment like she's about to argue. Then she tilts her head, matching his position. "Candles are fine, but my shirt stays on."

Charlie grunts his dissatisfaction but relinquishes with a subtle nod. Based on his reaction, he's utterly obsessed with her tits and stomach. I know him well enough that he'll spend most of the time kissing and touching every inch of her sweet, soft skin.

Bea's voice brings my attention back to her. "Masks stay on." Her voice trembles a little, and my body reacts. Wrapping an arm around her chest, I gently cup her jaw in my hand, stroking the pulse point on her neck.

Need laces through my tone, and I have to concentrate on keeping my voice steady. "It'll be hard to worship this body without our mouths, baby girl." A shiver races through her body, and I grin. "What about a blindfold?"

She considers this for the briefest moment, her eyes pinging around the room. The four of us must make a terrifying sight in our creepy masks and dark clothes. I briefly wonder if it's too much, too creepy. But eventually, she nods and grins sheepishly. "Ok," she whispers.

I stroke my thumb across the pulse on her neck and nod toward the nightstand near the bed. Danny immediately swipes the blindfold from the drawer and prowls toward us. Holding his hand out, she shakily slips the blindfold away from him. Over her shoulder, I can see her eyes widen with desire as she hones in on the dark holes covering his eyes, and his breathing stutters. *Yeah, man, I get it. Having her eyes bore into yours is life-changing.*

Turning out of my grasp and moving behind me, she turns off the leading lights, casting the room in a sensual glow from the candles flickering around. I shift my body and watch as she unclips her mask, slips it off her head, and places it on the small table by the door. A few moments later, the silky, black blindfold is securely tied behind her head.

She slowly turns back around to face us, and I watch her body play out the war in her mind. She stands up straight, then hunches slightly with uncertainty. She bites her lip and tugs her shirt down further on her waist, pinching it in the middle to, I assume, make sure it's not molding to her belly.

Needing to get her out of her own head, I nod at Stu, and he approaches slowly. Stepping over to her, I caution, "I'm just going to make sure it's tight enough." My voice is heavy with desire, and I quickly tighten the blindfold, then wriggle the material down her nose a little more.

Once I'm satisfied she can't see anything, I step back and look around to see the others begin taking off their masks. I follow, setting down the headphones and ripping off my mask. I set them on the table beside hers before facing the others. Glancing around quickly, I'm not surprised by what I see; A heavy mixture of lust and protectiveness shines through every gaze I meet.

Focusing back on Bea, I watch Stu slowly step up behind her, causing her to gasp in surprise. Putting his hands on her hips, he draws small, slow circles with his thumbs, dips his head into the juncture of her neck, and inhales deeply.

A tiny whimper escapes her as she leans her head away from Stu, allowing him to have access to her soft, perfect neck. *Can necks be perfect? Fuck if I know, but hers sure is.*

"Remind everyone of your safeword, baby girl. If we don't start in the next five seconds, I'm going to lose my mind." The last part comes out more like a snarl, and I watch with satisfaction as she presses her thighs together.

"Pink Unicorn." She moans out as Stu takes his long tongue and makes a path up her neck, straight to her ear.

"Good girl," I whisper before taking her hand and leading her to the massive bed. The bed is a beautiful, four-poster, California King-sized work of art. The sheets are bright red and made of bamboo instead of the typical silk. We chose the room because the bed will easily fit us all, and it has a bathroom attached.

Her breath hitches as her knees meet the edge of the bed, and I feel my smirk grow wide. "On the bed, baby girl. On your back."

Her body trembles beautifully as she plants her hands on the bed, sticking her ass out just a little before climbing up and crawling slowly across the sheets.

A loud *smack* echoes out over the soft playing music. She yelps and immediately turns her body, slamming her back on the bed.

Charlie's eyes sparkle with mischief and dominance as he leans over the bed and greedily takes her in. "He gave you an order, baby. Next time, your punishment for not obeying immediately will be worse." The low intensity of his voice causes Stu and Bea to both shiver.

"Yes, sir." She whispers. I can tell she's riding the adrenaline current of fear vs. pleasure, and I am all too excited to guide her down the river.

"Good girl," He croons softly, clearly picking up how much those two words affect her.

Straightening up, he stands over her and rolls his gaze all over her body. In fact, we all do. Stu is still at the end of the bed with me, Charlie is standing to the left, and Danny is to the right. Each of our bodies is wound tight and ready to strike.

But we don't. None of us moves. None of us speaks. We all stand there and watch as the gorgeous woman squirms under our perusal. The anticipation is building up so tightly in her body that I wouldn't be surprised if she...

"P-please," She whimpers. Her thighs rub together deliciously as the four of us stand over our little prey. *I knew she'd beg.*

"Please, what, my flower?" Danny hums teasingly as he begins shucking his shirt and shoes.

The rest of us follow.

Bea is quiet as she shifts under our gaze. She really hates asking for things, but she needs to learn the real power she has over us.

With a knowing look at Charlie, he smirks and rubs his hands together. Then, fast as lightning, he brings his large hand down on the top of her jean-clad pussy; just allowing his fingers to strike. She jumps and squeals in shock, but Charlie doesn't give her a second to overthink. "D asked you a question. Please, what? What does your beautiful body need?" His tone transforms from stern and dominating to almost a gentle purr. I mean, if lions can gently purr.

She mewls before stuttering out, "P-please. T-touch me." Her voice goes from lust-filled to self-conscious real damn quick. "Unless you don't want to. Just tell me, and we can end the scene. It's fi-"

I cut off her rambling by shooting over to the other side of the bed, grabbing her wrists, and slamming them above her head. "No," I growl in her ear. "You are *ours*. And we will take our sweet ass time worshiping this sexy body the way you deserve. Even if it means drawing out every ounce of your pleasure by edging you for the rest of the night." My voice sounds scratchy, and I know she can hear the pent-up desire in it.

I don't even give her a moment to respond. Instead, I put both wrists in one hand, holding them together and keeping them above her head on the bed. The movement creates a beautiful arch, and I knead her breast with my other hand. She mewls and writhes in response, and I signal for Stu to grab the handcuffs we had placed on the tiny nightstand.

Quickly securing both wrists, he threads the chain in the middle onto the carabiner right above her head. The metallic clinking increases as she undulates beneath us, causing my desire for her to spike. Her body arches into my roaming hand as she tests the cuffs for weaknesses, and her lip trembles with trepidation. "No touching for you today, baby girl. This is all about you."

With a quick glance at the others, I nod for them to join us on the bed, ready for the fun to really begin.

~CHAPTER 27~

Beatrice

The deliciously familiar bite of the cold metal around my wrists heightens my fear and my desire. For a brief moment, I hear shuffling around me but no one speaks. The sounds of belts coming undone, and zippers unzipping blast through the room like gunshots.

Wildest Dreams by Taylor Swift plays softly in the background; which is oddly perfect. I never in my wildest dreams would have thought I would be at the center of attention of four of the creepiest, sexiest men I've ever laid eyes on. Granted, I don't know what they *really* look like, but their terrifying masks, their confident stances, their dominating auras... *Hot dang! Can you have an orgasm without being touched??*

With the blindfold covering my vision, I struggle to stay present. The horrific feeling of being completely out of control and at the mercy of these men is completely scarousing. You know, equal parts scary and arousing. But I still have to focus on calming my racing heart. Either that or I'm going to have a heart attack. And *that* would just be embarrassing.

A warm, wet tongue dips near my clavicle, tracing a path up my neck towards my ear, and gently nibbles. His scent is crisp and clean; like charcoal soap with menthol. It's heady, yet oddly familiar. I feel his smooth skin and groan out as he sucks the lobe into his mouth with a rumbling moan as if I'm the tastiest treat he's ever had. My pussy clenches and I can feel my arousal pooling in my jeans.

A voice from the other side startles me momentarily. "Did you follow my directions like a good girl?" E's voice sends tingles straight to my core and I momentarily forget what his directions were.

A large hand palms my breast roughly before slowly making a pathway over my shirt. I cringe and try to suck in as he faintly traces a line down my stomach before I feel the cool air hit a tiny sliver of my belly. His fingers stop right at the top of my jeans; the tips slipping just underneath but not going any further. I thrust my hips up, already so on edge that the possibility of combusting seems highly probable.

"Tell me? Did you follow directions?" His voice is sterner this time, and I have to fight through the lust filling my brain to remember what he's talking about.

"Y-yes. N-no panties." I pant out. Male groans fill the room, causing me to become delirious with confidence from knowing I affect them at least half as much as they affect me.

A delicious mouth starts peppering kisses along my neck at the same time my pants are unzipped. My flats fall to the floor as my pants are ripped off of my legs with an urgency that makes my toes curl.

Then, hands descend all over my body. A mixture of rough and smooth fingertips touches every exposed inch of my skin. My brain short-circuits as the sensations overwhelm me and arousal leaks down my thighs. Nerve endings are firing faster than my brain can process.

Until someone lifts my shirt.

I suck in a deep breath, feeling as if ice water was suddenly dumped over my body. I desperately try sucking in my stomach as I scream out, "Shirt on!"

A delectably smooth, sensual voice glides over my other ear like icing on a cinnamon roll. "Your shirt is still on, flower. You never said we couldn't lift it to expose these juicy breasts."

He follows up his statement by scraping his teeth across my pulse. At the same time, someone else massages my breast through my bra, and four large hands begin trailing along my body. All 4 are rough to the touch, but one pair uses gentle pressure to glide up my legs from my knees, while the other pair of hands works his hands down my sides, starting from below my breasts. As the 2 pairs of hands get closer towards the part of my body that is aching for them, one man sucks in my earlobe and another sucks the skin on the other side of my neck. A highly indecent moan rips from my chest and I'm momentarily stunned stupid.

Icing voice chuckles and lays kisses across my jaw, dangerously close to my lips. Turning my head away, I silently remind him of my rule. Not that I think guys particularly enjoy kissing but, you know.

"What the fuck is that?" Everything seems to freeze in time. My breaths come out in harsh pants like I'm seconds from a cardiac event.

The two hands that are at the top of my thighs dig deep into my skin, causing me to squeak from the force.

"B... what is this?" The growly voice isn't E and hovers near my stomach area.

The two hands that were traveling down my sides suddenly disappeared. A single, rough finger trails down the side of my right hip, right over my fresh cuts. I flinch from the small, biting pain. *Oh, fork! I forgot about those. Wait...it's none of their concern.*

"I, um, it's nothing." I stammer out, trying and failing to sound firm in my conviction while simultaneously trying to process the whiplash from flying high and overwhelmed to dipping low and overwhelmed.

The melted icing voice responds with such a deep, sexual undertone that I feel my pussy clench around nothing. "Is my precious flower into knife play?"

His scent is leathery mixed with eucalyptus. It's a strange combination, but it matches his bedroom voice; overpowering and erotic. I swear to everything holy that he could have asked me if he could cut off my left leg and I would respond with the same answer. "Y-yes." I moan, arching my back.

The odd thing is, I'm not. My cuts aren't kink-related. They're to help ground me. But, they don't need to know that.

His answering groan vibrates through my body and I'm done for. It pains me to admit, I'm willing to pretend to like anything just so I can hear that sound again.

Suddenly, it's like someone pushes 'play' on the scene. My thighs are wrenched wide and a hot tongue swipes me from ass to clit. I try to pull back, squeaking in surprise. But, I can't go anywhere since a large arm clamps across my lower belly, effectively preventing me from moving.

"Oh my God!" I scream as whoever's between my legs begins to attack my clit with fervor. Someone near me flips my bra down, exposing my nipples to the cool room. Another mouth sucks a hickey on my neck.

I'm drowning in sensations, struggling hard against the cuffs that are digging painfully into my wrists. But the thrill of being chained up and at their mercy overrides any sense of fear.

A thick finger enters me and a rumbling groan vibrates through my clit as my pussy clenches down on it. My whole body shakes uncontrollably as another hand pinches my nipple, and yet another joins his friend between my legs. The devilish tongue moves to make room so his friend's fingers can scoop up some of my arousal, then rub it around and over my clit.

The finger in my pussy disappears, causing me to weep in frustration. To my surprise, two fingers replace it and begin to thrust into me almost violently. An orgasm starts to build as I thrash and pant.

It's so close, so spectacularly within reach, that I barely notice the sweet lips slowly making their way toward my mouth. His tongue sneaks out, tracing the very bottom of my lower lip. Then, four things happen at once: 1) Two hands tweak both nipples, 2) A third finger is added to the others and they all curl forward, 3) Someone pinches my clit, and 4) My lower lip is sucked into someone's mouth and he bites down before I can object.

But, I instantly forget it all.

Stars burst behind the blindfold and my whole body locks up as the most intense orgasm rushes through my body. There's a high-pitched ringing in my ears, and I think tears are drenching my blindfold, but I can't be sure. It feels like electricity is being pushed through my whole body in shockwaves before morphing into something surreal.

I feel like I'm floating; like my soul is leaving my body. Everything twitches and tingles, before going numb.

~CHAPTER 28~

Beatrice

What feels like an eternity later, I feel myself floating back to Earth. The ringing in my ears is still there, but I can hear the faint murmurs of the men around me cooing and calming me, their hands gently rubbing down my arms, legs, chest, and hair. It's *forking* amazing.

"You with us, my precious flower? I have a bottle of water with a straw for you. That was so damn hot." He groans, and at the same time, I feel a plastic straw brush against my lips. I suck the cool liquid down greedily, immediately relieved as the cooling sensation surges through my body.

"Good girl," the deep, throaty voice says across the room. I didn't even hear him step away. I wonder if it belongs to the guy in the red and black Jason mask.

After I drink, I lick my lips with anticipation, knowing that these men clearly aren't finished, even though they've made me a hot mess. Still, anticipation buzzes through my veins as I try to control my breathing.

"Are you ready for us? Now that we've got you nice and dirty?" E's deep growl sounds similar to how it sounded in the forest, and I feel a gush of arousal leak down my ass crack. *Not cute.*

"Y-yes, sir." My brain isn't fully functioning yet, and I sound more like a scared mouse than a horny slut, but whatever. It's their fault.

The chuckles around me are deep, dark, and filled with a type of masculinity that only sex gods can pull off.

Shuffling my legs closed, I realize no one is on the bed with me. The last song ends, and the next one immediately begins. The sexy melody of Lana Del Rey's Lust for Life creates an erotic soundtrack and does nothing to help the feelings threatening to burst from my chest.

Someone turns it down, just a tad, causing me to squirm even more. The otherwise silence in the room is making me uncomfortable, giving me just enough time to realize that I'm naked from my bra down, my shirt is still rucked up around my neck, and I'm handcuffed.

Adrenaline and embarrassment threaten to knock me out. My head feels light and fuzzy, and my heart rate picks up. Before I know it, I'm panicking again. My lip trembles with anxiety, and I move to curl in on myself to hide from their judgmental eyes.

"Ah, ah, ah, baby girl. You're ours, now, which means we get to look at this sexy body as long as we want to." E's voice comes directly from my left, startling me from my panic attack. My hands jangle against the cuffs, causing a metallic pinging to echo out.

Without no additional comments, two very different hands grab my ankles and push my feet up towards my ass. Something like fuzzy cloth is secured around each ankle, and I realize I'm officially strapped down to the bed.

"Spread your knees." The growly voice runs over me like sweet molasses, and I whimper, following the command immediately. Two more hands lift my ass, and some kind of small wedge pillow slides under my back; leaving my ass and naughty bits on full display as my knees fall to the side.

"Good girl. That's my good, dirty girl." The rumbling quality of E's voice has me clenching on nothing, and I begin to shake as the anticipation of what they are going to do heightens.

But, with the new angle of my hips and my hands cuffed behind my head and raised a little, I'm having a hard time breathing. And I think a nerve is pinched in my right shoulder, which is causing my hand to go numb.

"Um..." I whisper, scared to ruin the scene.

Licking my lips, I try again, "Y-yellow. Please."

E's lust-filled voice rings out, but there's a seriousness to it now. "Paused. What do you need, baby girl?" I can hear him shuffle up the side of the bed, and his voice moves with him.

"The, uh, the angle...I like it, but it's kind of hard to breathe with my hands up. And my right hand is going numb. I think I punched a nerve."

I barely finish my sentence, and hands descend on me, rubbing up and down my arms, massaging my shoulders, unclasping the handcuffs, and releasing me. It's a whirlwind of activity, and I breathe a sigh of relief as my arms fall. Long, smooth hands work on my shoulders, rubbing my arms and helping with circulation.

After all the pins and needles from the numbness go away, I whisper, "Thank you." Emotions clog my throat, and I have to choke them down. This is one of the reasons I don't do aftercare. It's too...nice...sweet...addicting.

Thankfully, I don't have time to get lost in terrified feelings as the growly, molasses voice speaks from between my legs. "Are you ready to start again or do you need to safeword?"

I'm already shaking my head vehemently. "No. I'm good. I'm ready." I say with what I hope is a coy smile.

"OK, baby, but I want to check in. I know the last position got uncomfortable, but do you think you can handle being cuffed to the bed with your hands down, maybe spread out a little, instead of above?"

The images that flit through my brain shoot a new wave of lust through my body. "Yes, please," I moan.

Within ten seconds, I'm strapped much more comfortably to the bed, arms down and spread a little like an upside-down V. The straps are the same soft, fuzzy material as those around my ankles. I test the bindings to ensure they aren't too tight but still restrictive.

Honestly, they're perfect.

"Scene," E calls out. I smile, barely able to contain my excitement.

Before E explains what's coming next.

~CHAPTER 29~

Even

This woman has all of us tied up by the balls and she has no idea. Charlie looks at her like she made his favorite gun by hand, Danny fidgets like he's considering tying her up in our own bed to prevent her from leaving, and Stu... well, Stu looks like he's going to cry, or crack and give himself away.

Clearing my throat, I walk to stand between Bea's gorgeous, milky thighs. Her pussy is a pink, quivering, sopping mess. I grip the base of my cock for a second, biting my lip to ward off having a damn orgasm before she has another one. We have a plan. Tonight is all about her.

Slipping back into my Dom persona, I take a deep breath and grin down at the beauty before me. "Mmmm, baby girl, look at this lonely pussy. Guys, have you seen a more beautiful pussy in your life?"

The others take my lead and strut over. We crowd around her open legs and watch in delight as her thighs quake in anticipation. The little hot pockets on the insides of her thighs beg to be touched, squeezed, licked, and bit. *Focus!*

With a quick glance at the others, I give them a subtle nod to proceed with the plan. We all descend on her with one hand each. None of us rush our movements, but we don't stay in one spot long.

I slowly trace a trail from her pussy to her cute little asshole. She gasps in surprise and I circle it with my digit. Meanwhile, Danny's tracing lazy patterns on the left side of her slit, never quite hitting her pussy, or her clit. Stu's standing the furthest away and is using that to his advantage as he draws slow circles and lines around her hood, dipping in occasionally to meet the flesh inside but never crossing her clit. Charlie mirrors Danny. Not quite in sync, but he's staying to the outside or very inside of her plush lips; never dipping all the way down.

We all continue our slow ministrations and watch as she unfolds for us. She tries to lift her hips but it's almost impossible with the wedge under her delectable ass.

Danny watches intensely as my fingers draw tight circles around her ass; his eyes lit up with desire. "D, suck my fingers. Get them nice and wet so I can slip them into our girl's tight ass." Beatrice groans out, then stops suddenly.

Her whole body tenses and I see her noticeably try to clench her ass cheeks together. "What?!" She shrieks.

Danny makes a filthy, over-the-top slurping sound and groans as I fuck my two fingers into his mouth like I would my cock. "What's the matter, baby girl?" I barely finish as I groan at the mixture of the feeling of Danny's mouth on my fingers and the blazing hot look he's trapped me in.

Clearing my throat, I free my fingers and look down at Bea. "Have you ever had someone touch this cute little ass?" I damn near growl thinking of someone else having had her this way, but I know I can't dwell on that.

"Um, y-yes." Her tremulant, hushed voice causes me to pause and take her in. Her lip is quivering and she looks like she's trying to hunch in on herself. That's all I needed to see to know it wasn't by her fucking choice.

White hot rage rushes over me and I feel my muscles lock up. A quick glance at the others tells me that they see it, too. Stu, however, is what really gives it away. His face is a mixture of agony and sympathy. *He knows.*

For a moment, it hangs awkwardly in the air around us.

But, thank God for Danny. He crawls up the bed like a little puppy and gives her feather-light kisses across her jaw and neck. After she relaxes a little, he whispers loud enough for us to hear. "If you want to pass, you can, but if anyone can make it feel good, it's E."

He glances at me out of the corner of his eye, smirking. This little shit is about to tease us both. "You know all those piercings his dick has?"

She thrusts her hips a little, moans, then gasps. "Uh-huh." The sweet, sexy sound causes my dick to jump eagerly. But, I force my body to remain still.

"Well, all of those piercings have been allll up inside of *me*." He groans and thrusts his cock against her thigh. "It f-feels so damn good. He knows how to make it feel good. And he'll always start s-slow with you."

He moans deep in his chest and I lean over to see that he apparently got close enough to her hand that she's now stroking him. "F-fuuckk. Your hands are so soft. So, fucking perfect. My precious flower." His hips twitch as she moves her hand over his length.

I take her silence as temporary permission until she says otherwise. Since the air has dried off most of Danny's spit, I pop open the lube bottle next to me. Applying a generous amount, I flip the lid closed and nudge my finger at her entrance.

Glancing over at Charlie, I tilt my chin, silently giving him the go-ahead. With a mischievous grin, he slowly starts circling her clit, and she moans like a filthy vixen. When her body becomes soft and compliant, I gently prod my finger into her tight hole; moving in and out slowly so she can adjust the size and feel.

After her tension fades, and she begins fucking our hands, I up the ante. "Ok, baby girl. We're going to play a game."

I peer over at Stu with a raised brow, ensuring he's still on board. In response, he smirks and crawls onto the bed. He begins massaging one of her perfectly plump breasts. Then his mouth leans in and his long-ass tongue starts to flick her nipple.

I'm completely mesmerized as Beatrice unravels; moaning and panting with need. "The rules are: If you answer a question truthfully, we keep doing what we're doing. But, if you lie, or you don't answer, you get punished."

She squeaks in protest but continues to stroke Danny's hard cock and pushes her chest deeper into Stu's mouth.

With a grin, I hand Charlie the flower vibrator from the side of the bed and drip a little more lube onto my fingers. Not wanting to give her time to protest, I slide my finger out of her back hole and immediately begin carefully inserting two; twisting them back and forth to ease them in. At the exact same time, my other hand moves in and I enter one finger into her soaking wet pussy.

She tries to buck at the intrusion but the angle of her hips prevents it. Her head is shaking like she's overwhelmed already and I chuckle darkly. "Hold on tight, baby girl. You're in for a ride."

Stu groans deeply, his chest vibrating with the sound as he finally scoots close enough for her to grab onto his dick. "Holy schnitzel! Are you all forking pierced?" She heaves while her whole body quivers.

Danny's fucking himself with her hand and pinches her nipple while Stu is content with letting her set the pace while he licks and sucks her breast.

Charlie clicks the button for the vibrator, hovering just above her sweet clit. I don't even know if she can hear it above the low music playing and the sounds the three of them are making.

"First question," I bark out, ensuring I have her attention. I decided to go easy on the first couple of questions, so she's really worked up for us.

"Did you like it when D sucked my fingers and talked about me fucking him in the ass?" Her sultry groan appears to vibrate from the deepest part of her soul. "Yes!" She pants.

Her two holes are squeezing me so damn hard as I stroke them in and out of her tight holes. Charlie places the clit-sucking vibrator onto her barely-there nub while holding her hood open with his other hand.

"OH GOD!" She screams. Her movements on Stu and Danny's cocks stutter and the veins in her neck look like they may just burst. They groan out and I can only assume she's squeezing them tight.

"Fuuucckk," Charlie groans. "You're so damn responsive, baby. So fucking hot." He grits out, dropping his hand from her hood in favor of stroking his dick.

"Second question," I grit my teeth as her pussy and ass clench around my fingers so tightly that I wonder if my cock will explode in response. "Why did you say you didn't need aftercare?" I'm trying to remember my point but her ass and pussy are squeezing me so tight that it's hard to concentrate.

"Wh-what? Why?" She asks between breaths.

Then, we all stop. Like a well-oiled machine, every finger, hand, device, and cock drops away from her. Her answering whine is equal parts sad and sexy. She tosses her head back against the bed and blows a raspberry in frustration. It's fucking adorable.

"Answer the question." With a half growl, she shakes her head repeatedly, lifting her hips as if something will magically appear.

Eventually, she realizes we really did back away, she huffs in annoyance. "It's a waste of time. Why have someone do all that when I can get back to my own house and take care of my dang self?"

Yes! Her fire has been ignited. That sass I've learned to crave comes out, and I grin. I'm happy she's playing along. *Of course, she's not going to be happy in a second.*

With a glance at Charlie, I turn the punishment over to him. His eyes sparkle mischievously as he steps up. Quick as a whip, his hand swiftly comes down on her exposed pussy and she yelps in response. "I said no lies, baby girl. I'm a patient man, but I don't tolerate liars."

She whimpers pitifully and faces the opposite wall, so I push a little more. "You're well-versed in BDSM, baby girl. Aftercare is just as important as the boundaries and the scene itself. I know you know this. So, why skip that part?"

With a deep breath, she whispers the words just loud enough that we can hear. Her words are calculated, specific, and heartbreakingly clear: this woman has worked hard to protect herself. "I don't like aftercare because it's too intimate, too personal. Sub-drop feels very similar to most of my life so, *that,* I can handle. I just can't handle my heart getting involved. I know better." Her voice is almost non-existent by the time she finishes, and just like that, we've learned a little more about our girl.

"Thank you for being honest, baby girl." I finish my statement and plunge two fingers deep into her wet pussy. She screams out with a mixture of shock and pleasure as her pussy grips me; like it's trying to keep me there. Her back arches, just a little off the bed, and I feel her try to slip away. Thankfully, between the wedge pillow and the restraints, she isn't going anywhere.

"Open up my precious flower," Danny coos, rubbing his hands through her hair. She immediately obeys, flicking her tongue out to play with the dydoe piercing on top of his tip. After a few explorative licks and twirls, she takes his dick in her mouth, simultaneously reaching for Stu.

I glance up at Charlie, who's squeezing the base of his dick hard. He must feel my gaze on him as he meets my eyes. Squinting at him while I continue fucking her with my fingers, he shakes his head, silently telling me he's waiting for the right moment to add the vibrator again.

Stu grunts, bringing my gaze back to him in time to watch her use her thumb to spread his pre-cum over his tip and then down the barbells of his Jacobs Ladder. Bea's head bobs across Danny's thickness, and she laps at him like she's starving. My dick is so hard that I have to press into the bed just to find a modicum of relief while trying to match her rhythm and movements; fucking her like she's sucking Danny.

Stu makes a strangled sound. I look over and see that Stu is wide-eyed as her nails scrape along the piercings lining the underside of his cock. I have to bite my cheek to prevent myself from laughing. *He's totally about to blow.*

Her squeals, moans, and grunts of pleasure- muffled by Danny's thick cock- along with the sound of her wet pussy gushing from all the attention is a beautiful sound. I desperately wish I could record it and play it every damn day.

"Next question, baby girl," I grit out; the pain in my balls is becoming almost unbearable. She whimpers around Danny's thick cock and shakes her head in defiance.

I have to almost force my fingers out as her greedy little pussy tries to keep them locked in. Once I succeed, I hear her harumph of annoyance.

With a clearing of my throat, everyone immediately slows their movement. This time, we all glide across her skin gently, with barely-there touches along her hips, legs, arms, and lips... she squirms in frustration, and I can see tears leaking from the edge of her blindfold.

Danny leans down and licks her trail of tears up before rasping, "Don't cry, Flower; I promise we'll be good to you."

I've never seen Danny become so infatuated so quickly. Not that it was any different for me.

"Last question, I promise," I groan out, sticking one finger in her sweet pussy and lazily pumping in and out as Charlie barely brushes across her clit. Her panting for air reminds me of the night in the forest and I grunt in appreciation.

I add a second digit, lazily slipping in and out of her as Charlie gently massages her breasts, her neck, her arms. Stu and Danny simultaneously move in and sweetly kiss along her neck and jaw.

"This one has two parts." She groans in petulant frustration and Charlie brings his hand down on her pussy with a loud smack. Her whole body jolts, and she takes in a sharp inhale, right before I feel her needy cunt grip my fingers tighter. "Goddamn. You liked that, baby girl?"

"No!" She exclaims indignantly. Charlie slaps her pussy again; this time adding in a faint circle around her clit before moving away.

"Your tight little cunt says you're a liar," I respond matter-of-factly.

"Fine, yes....Please!" She thrust her hips towards me, desperate for more attention.

"Ok, baby girl. First part of the question: You said your happiest memory was meeting a friend, now ex-friend, that he betrayed you. What did he do?"

Her whole body goes still. I quickly shoot knowing looks at everyone, making sure they don't stop their slow perusal. She needs help relaxing, trusting, and sharing; so that's what we're going to help her with.

Stu gently lavishes her neck with small nibbles and Danny helps her stroke his dick almost absentmindedly. Charlie leans down and flicks his tongue lazily over her nipple. I keep up my ministrations, pumping, twisting, scissoring; oh, *so*, slowly.

She whimpers out. Her chest rises and falls harshly as she loses herself to the sensations and battles her mind for the answer.

For about fifteen seconds, we keep up the slow, torturous pace, with nothing but our harsh pants echoing around us. Her whole body begins to quiver as the sensations slowly drive her mad. Only then does she start to divulge.

"He, uh, he broke my trust." She licks her lips before biting down on her bottom one.

Stu kisses her jaw and runs his fingers through her hair, causing her to gasp and mewl loudly. I'm a little afraid he's about to lose it. His eyes are closed and his face is pinched with pain. But, she doesn't know that, so she goes on. "He knows I don't trust people. Only him. Only him for years and, uh..." her breathing is becoming heavier again as we all slowly up our tempo with each muttered confession.

"I got hurt. And he and some guys saved me. But they were in my hous-" she breaks off on a guttural groan as I insert a lubed finger into her cute little ass.

"Ok, so he helped. Sounds like a good thing." I'm gritting my teeth so hard that I fear they may crack. My resolve is slowly withering.

"N-no. I don't trust people. He knew that and he, he, showed them a secret place." She moans and begins to rotate her hips, fucking herself on my fingers. Her cheeks flush brighter and her whole body starts to quake with her impending orgasm.

She's right on the edge. She just needs a little push. "But if you could trust him with secrets like that, don't you think you can trust his decision on who to bring over? Especially if they were there to help?" I implore; pumping my fingers into her much faster.

"N-no. He broke my trust. Oooo! That's it.... Right there... Oh God..." Something between a whine and a groan slips through her gritted teeth and she digs her nails into Stu's and Danny's forearms.

I add a third finger to her pussy and a second to her ass and she chokes on a moan. "P-please." Tears fall from underneath her mask and she thrashes her head as we bring her to the edge again.

"You're doing so good, baby, so fucking sexy. Almost there. Do you want me to vibrate that little clitty for you? She looks so needy and alone." Charlie's thick voice glides across the room like a sensual wave and I almost cum all over the bed.

"Y-yes, p-please." Her cries match the quaking of her body as the others continue their deeper perusals of her body.

"Last question and then I'll take the vibrator and latch it onto your clit. E will fuck you with his fingers so good, that you'll cease to exist. I'll mark this breast, here, while D marks that one. And S will make sure that sexy neck of yours is taken care of." We all groan and grunt in response and Bea nods her head adamantly.

"Why did the betrayal feel so bad that you ended the friendship?" I look up and see Stu with tears in his eyes as he tries to focus on every erogenous zone he can find.

She shakes her head violently, refusing to answer. "I can't." She whispers.

Instead of everyone stopping, Charlie flicks on the flower, the vibrating sound barely penetrating the room as whatever song plays softly. He licks her stiff nipple and places the bud against it. Bea thrashes wildly as he clicks the button again.

"Doesn't that feel good, dirty girl?" She groans, arching her back and pressing her breast into the toy. "Think how good it would feel on your clit. Sucking on it like it's a damn treat; vibrating the entire little bundle until your toes curl and you cream all over E's hands."

A long, high-pitched moan I've never heard before quivers through her chest as her whole body starts to tremble like she's seizing.

Just when I think we will have to move away, she screams, "I fell in love with him, ok? And I don't do that. I can't do that. Ohhhh, G-god!!!"

Charlie immediately pops the toy off of her breast and quickly latches it to her clit. I pump my fingers in and out of her, making sure to hit that rough bundle of nerves deep inside her pussy. Danny bites down on her collarbone, and Stu latches on her mouth, kissing her with a ferocity I've never seen from him.

And then, the mother of all orgasms rips through her body. Her neck bows damn near completely underneath her. Danny groans deeply as crimson trails of blood flow from where her nails are embedded in his arm. Her scream bounces off the walls as her upper body becomes completely covered in a deep, sweaty blush. Her feet tense along with her legs, and her pussy clenches painfully around my fingers. We all keep working her through it as pulsing waves thrum through her body almost violently.

A familiar push from her pussy reminds me of what she did in the forest, and I quickly remove my fingers. Charlie keeps the toy on her clit and she sucks in a loud gasp. Her mouth opens in a wide O, and she goes almost completely still, as gush, after sexy fucking gush, floods out of her body; soaking me and the mattress beneath us.

I'm transfixed by the sight before me but am quickly brought back as she makes gasping sounds like she's having trouble breathing.

Reading her body cues, Charlie sees that she's hit the breaking point at the same time I do. He immediately removes the vibrator, clicks it off, and tosses it on the floor. Then, we all gather around her, petting her calmly with loving touches.

Danny chuckles and nuzzles her neck, "Oh silly flower, I already marked your belly when you drew blood with those pretty nails. So hot..." he coos, licking up her neck and causing her to shiver. A shift of her lips tells me she's trying to grin but is just too damn exhausted to do so.

"Good." She whispers and nuzzles him back.

I assume she was trying to stroke him to completion. Sweet woman. Always thinking of others.

My dick is still hard as steel in my hand as I stroke it, "Gunna mark you with our cum, baby girl." I grunt as my balls already begin to tingle with need.

She lifts her hands to help but Charlie stops her before I can, "No, no, baby. You're the perfect, creamy canvas for us to paint our cum on." His deep growl comes from somewhere deep within and makes him sound more monster than man.

Stu's still quiet while he strokes his cock, as planned, but leans down and kisses her again. Like he just can't help it. Like he's trying to pour every apology and every ounce of love into the kiss. Their tongues lazily dancing with each other is like watching a Greek tragedy. It's heartbreakingly beautiful.

The three of us groan our release simultaneously and splash our cum on her belly, on top of where Danny's load was already waiting.

Sated, relieved, and deliriously fucking happy, we all collapse on the bed, collectively trying to cool off and catch our breaths.

After a minute of silence, we wordlessly move and begin unstrapping the fuzzy bindings around her ankles and wrists, briefly rubbing the areas to help her limbs regain circulation. Charlie carefully lifts her hips and I push out the wedge beneath her so she can lie flat on the bed. Then, we all lie around her. Our fingers trace across her legs, arms, neck, anywhere we can touch, as we all fall into a comfortable silence.

After some time passes, Stu rolls off the bed and walks towards the bathroom, turning on the bath. Following him in, I clean off the remnants of mine and Bea's releases and watch as he fills the bath with Lavender Epsom Salt; then turns to me. His eyes brim with tears but his smile is a silent "thank you" that I didn't even need. With an understanding nod, I turn and go back to the bed.

Charlie slips off the mattress as I snuggle in behind Danny, groaning against his neck and relishing in this moment of connection with him. He hums in response and locks my arms around his chest.

Bea's soft snores raise my eyebrows, and I'm shocked to see Charlie smiling down at her. He's probably the most like Beatrice in our group, and I momentarily wonder if they may be perfect for each other.

Charlie bends down, scooping Bea up in his arms, and whispers, "Wake up, baby. Gotta get you cleaned up." He gently kisses her cheek and she jolts in surprise.

Then, all hell breaks loose.

~CHAPTER 30~

Beatrice

The warm embrace of darkness surrounds me like my favorite weighted blanket. I feel like I'm floating in the air as the darkness recedes ever so slightly.

A deep, velvety voice arouses me from my dream-like state. "...cleaned up," is all I manage to hear before the sweetest forking kiss graces my cheek. *Wait, what?*

My eyes pop open, and I jolt from the contact. But everything is dark. So very dark. *Crap on a cracker. Where am I?*

I scream out and move to hit my attacker. All of my past terrors flash through my mind. "Woah, you're ok. You're safe."

The words barely register as I thrash and kick; realizing quickly that I have no gosh-darned pants on. "Screw you! Let me go!" I screech, clocking the man with the big arms and stupidly hard chest.

"Ok, ok. I'm going to let you down, but you've gotta stop, or you'll hurt yourself." I snarl in response but feel my body shifting in his arms, allowing me just enough freedom to jump to the floor. I land less than gracefully and wobble like a baby giraffe as I stand.

Thankfully, my arms and legs aren't bound, so I rip the mask away from my face. The light burns my eyes, causing me to squeeze them shut as I try to regain my equilibrium. Adrenaline floods my body. Somewhere deep in my fog-filled brain, I know I need to quickly get over the hazy feeling so I can find a way to escape.

"Beatrice, stop! It's us. You came to The Raven Room to meet us." The familiar voice floats into my panicked mind, momentarily calming me—until I realize he said my actual name. *They know my name!*

My eyes fly open, and I scan the room. Four men. Four very naked men stand around the room.

The dude to my left is a giant among men. His blonde hair is shaved close all over. He has a picturesque chiseled jaw that narrows before plateauing briefly at his chin. His nose is slight but fucking perfect underneath a pair of ice-blue eyes. He looks like he plays football; all built-up and intimidatingly sexy. He seems familiar, but I can't place him. Then again, I'm absolutely sucked in by the ridges of his abs and the sharp V of his Adonis Belt. *Damn, that V could be used to cut meat.*

My brain forgets to tell me to stop as my eyes travel lower. A thick erection stands proudly; showcasing his Prince Albert and lorum piercings.

Then it clicks.

I trace the lines of his forearms and stomach once again before glaring up at his stupidly perfect, dang face.

"Alpha!?!" I whisper, praying to God that I'm dreaming. Or maybe it's a nightmare. His smooth, slightly tanned cheeks redden, and I see the flash of guilt in his eyes.

Before I can question him, I see something shuffle from the corner of my eye. I back up a little, making sure I can still keep an eye on Alpha, and move to face two drool-worthy specimens. The first guy is close to me- about six feet away- and is built much like the man next to me. However, this man has tattoos adorning his hands, chest, and all down his arms. He's a deliciously fine work of art. The man to his right is just a few inches taller than him but has more lean muscle and sinew. Like his friend, tattoos decorate his arms; but his are filled with bright colors, whereas the other man's tats are mainly black and gray. The muscular man has a thick, soft-looking beard that scoops just a few inches off his chin but doesn't hit his collarbone. But, the leaner one has a smattering of black stubble that makes him look devilishly handsome.

When I reach their eyes, my perusal halts, and my heart races. I *know* those maple-colored eyes and have fantasized about running my hands through the black wavy locks perfectly framing the leaner man's face.

And the blue-green irises of the other man staring back at me have been in my dreams more than once in the last few weeks. His long, honey-colored hair is disheveled but still rests in a bun down his neck. They both have their hands out in a calming gesture, but their eyes are wide with, with... what *is that?* Fear? Guilt? Regret?

"Even! Danny?" I yell incredulously. "What- how?" Bile splashes at the back of my throat, and my vision tunnels with panic. *Danny and Even are here. How are they here? I met them with Stu. With Stu...*

Whipping my head to the far right, my heart lurches in my throat. Just outside of the bathroom door stands Stu. Gloriously naked for all to see. His shaggy, pink hair isn't as bright as it was a few weeks ago, and is sticking to his head with sweat.

His gorgeous bright blue eyes are sad, frightened; maybe even a little shocked. Unlike the others, he stands there with his shoulders curled in on himself; like he's resigned to being the butthead in this whole jacked-up scenario.

And, sue me, I'm in shock, so yes, I do openly take in every forking corded vein running down his slender arms. He's not as built as the others, more like a swimmer or runner, but hot dang, he's no less attractive. Scars litter his perfect, toned body, and I feel myself scowl indignantly. *Who the fork hurt him? I'll frigging kill 'em.*

And that's the thought that sends me spiraling. My brain decides to try to process too much information at once...

E is Even.
I've had sex with him twice.
Even and Danny and this other guy are all Stu's friend.
The other guy is Alpha—my video-sex friend.
Piercings. So many piercings.

Oh, forkballs! *The piercings. The piercings attached to the dick I stroked, which is attached to the man who forking kissed me, is Stu's!*

Even kissed me. Bad.
Stu kissed me. Worse.

I gasp aloud, my body feeling like a thousand tiny needles are stabbing me at once, and I almost faint at my next thought.

I admitted to loving Stu.

Even steps forward like he's going to say something but I put my hand up to stop him. "N-no. No, no, no, no. Back up. Just stop."

After a brief look around, I locate the mask I wore here, and my pants. I snatch the pants off the floor and quickly shove my legs into them before zipping them up.

"Beatrice, please stop! Let us explain." Alpha pleads. His growly voice rumbles through my body, and I feel my whorish pussy tingle.

But I don't. I can't.

Biting my lip hard to prevent my tears from spilling over, I scoop up my shoes, then my mask, and back up towards the door. My hand connects with the cool metal, and I almost weep in relief. Twisting the lock, I open it wide; the music from the club blasts through the bubble of Hell I'm currently standing in.

All of the men move to step forward, and I shake my head, tears falling down my face against my permission. Once I clear the doorway, I turn and run like my jiggly rear end is on fire.

"Bea-"

"Beatrice-"

"Bea-"

"Flower-"

I hear the desperation in their voice, but I ignore them.

Running down the hall, I hang a right and come out onto the main club floor. I don't stop, even as I near a trash can by the bar, and toss away my mask. My bare feet carry me through the black door and into the front lobby, where I shakily enter the pin to my locker to grab my things.

The manager calls out after me, but I can't stop. I need to leave. I have to get out of here. So I just wave and thank her out loud as I hit the release bar on the front door.

Flinging my backpack in front of me, I unzip it as I run. The tiny pebbles in the parking lot usually irritate my sensitive feet, but I have one focus: getting to my bike.

Halting next to my bike, I shake out my Dianese's, slip them on, and tie them up before flinging my flats into my backpack. I don't bother connecting my BlueTooth for music to the helmet, and I don't bother with my gloves. I just jump on, slide on my helmet, secure the strap, and insert my key.

The bike roars to life between my legs and rattles areas of my body I almost wish weren't sensitive and deliciously sore. Tears blur my vision as I pull out of my spot and rev down the aisle. The four men I left inside burst through the front door in just their pants; the rest of their clothing and boots in their arms, hiding most of their muscular forms.

My emotions are far too high, but I can't slow down; I can't stop. My breathing is uneven, and sobs keep getting caught in my throat. The street lights and headlights blur as my tears continue to fall.

This is my fault. I was selfish. I wanted one more night of bliss before ending it, and I got burned worse than ever. There is no coming back from this, and I don't want to.

Suddenly, a horn blares, and I fling my eyes open; not realizing I had shut them. It doesn't take long to match the horn sound with the giant truck coming my way. *Fork! I'm in the oncoming traffic lane!*

Panic consumes me, and I whip back into the right lane...

But, I overcorrect and lose control.

Skid. *thump thump*
Crunch. *thump thump*
Silver metal. *thump thump*
Horns blaring. *thump thump, thump thump*
Flying. *thump thump, thump thump, thump thump*
The ground rises to meet me. *thump thump, thump thu-*

~CHAPTER 31~

Stu

Four Days Later

I have a lot of regrets in life: letting my abusive ass uncle live, getting involved in the Black Diamonds when I was a teen, not buying stock in Samsung when they first started out...but my greatest regret is thinking this hair-brained idea would legitimately get Beatrice to finally *see* me, *know* me, *choose* me.

We rushed out of The Raven Room in time to watch her peel out of the parking lot. The look of absolute shame and betrayal on her face before she fled the club shattered my heart and soul.

But the sight we drove up to, barely three minutes later, obliterated both.

Traffic had just started backing up; a few people were rushing from their cars to peer over the dented guardrail; the pavement surrounding it littered with debris. Once I saw the commotion, I knew. We all knew.

Charlie slowed down and pulled over into the shoulder, and we all hopped out, sprinting towards the wreckage. Thankfully, we had already tossed on our shirts and just needed to slip on our shoes.

Rushing over to the growing crowd, whispers surrounded us. We quickly gathered that a bike was driving in the wrong lane. The rider overcorrected, lost control, and slid into the guardrail before flying over. My stomach heaved and I had to brace myself on Charlie's shoulder to keep me upright. His entire body vibrated, and I felt his muscles tensing beneath my palm. Usually, he hates touch, but he didn't bother shrugging me off. Maybe he needed grounding as much as I did.

A few people started sliding down the embankment, wrenching us out of our shock. Almost as one, we move to follow them down in search of the rider.

The embankment was steep but not so bad that we couldn't navigate the drop easily. The brush at the bottom covered most of the ground, making it impossible to see. The flashlights from all the phones lit up the area in sections as we all spread out.

After another painfully long minute, a dark figure caught our eye. Time seemed to slow down, but my feet carried me forward, faster and faster, towards the dark figure lying awkwardly on the ground.

"How's she doin'?" Charlie's voice startles me out of my memory. I feel my face form a frown as I try to remember where I am and what I'm supposed to be doing.

Swallowing thickly, I blink a few times and take in my surroundings.

Light gray painted walls with white decorative swirls decorate the top six inches of the walls around the room. I'm in the only sitting chair in the room, but there is a navy blue chaise lounge next to the far window overlooking the pool.

Deep gray bamboo sheets adorn the king-sized bed in the middle of the room and are covered by a Navy blue weighted blanket. Under that blanket is a lump known as Beatrice. But, she's not the sassy, sexy, stunning woman I've come to love. She's been unconscious for 4 days; since the night she went careening down an embankment.

Charlie shifts near me, reminding me that I haven't answered. Clearing my throat, I rub my palms down my pants and shift uncomfortably. "No change. Nothing better, nothing worse." I mumble.

His hum is non-committal as he slips his hands into his pockets; standing next to me like a quiet sentinel. The steady beeping of the heart rate monitor is the only sound in the room.

We got her out of the bushes, Charlie cradling her protectively to his chest until he was met with the paramedics at the top of the embankment. He struggled to hand her over to them but finally relinquished when they reminded him that every second was vital; and he was delaying her care.

Once the ambulance doors closed, we hopped in the truck and sped after them. Then we spent hours sitting in the small, cold waiting room, as she was rushed to surgery. Her left leg had shattered, and her right arm broke in 2 places from impact.

Her helmet saved her noggin, and I was momentarily grateful she had enough wherewithal to snap it in place before taking off.

But, the rest of her body, looked like a macabre Jackson Pollock. She was basically a giant bruise splattered with scrapes, cuts, and a gnarly ass road rash along the left side of her body.

Two days later, she was stable enough to be moved. We got Doc to sign off on transferring her to our place so we could keep an eye on her. It's our fault she ran, so we should take care of her. Since then, Doc has stopped by every 8 hours or so and given us updates and instructions as needed.

The light beeping of her heart rate monitor, and her soft, sweet snores are the only things keeping me going.

"Oh, uh, before I forget: This came for you today."

He slips out an envelope, just larger than my hand. It's thick and black with a silver seal stamped on the back. In the middle is a curly, gothic letter B.

Turning it over, I see that it's actually a note from Beatrice. My eyes widen and I glance up at her. She must have sent this before we all met that night. *Why didn't she just text or call me?*

Ripping it open, I pull out the letter and read Bea's words. Tears fall freely down my face as she pours out her soul to me.

But, the more I read, the more it becomes clear. This isn't a forgiveness letter; or even an apology letter.

She's saying goodbye.

Images of her haunted eyes, cut-up hips, and carefully curated persona flash through my mind. Beatrice was leaving me, leaving us; forever. She planned on killing herself even before she met with us that night.

My stomach heaves and its contents start to make their way up my throat.

Standing suddenly, I fight off the dizziness and latch on to anger, disappointment, and despair.

"Woah, there, Hacker. You okay?" Charlie steadies me with his hands on my hips as I slouch forward, trying to breathe.

"No," I grunt out as the room spins.

Slamming the now crumpled letter into his chest, I shove him away and run to the bathroom down the hall, trying to leave her words, her truth behind.

I barely make it to the toilet before I lose my lunch, and breakfast, for the day. I shouldn't have tossed the letter like that but, I couldn't form the words. I couldn't wrap my head around the actuality of what she was planning.

Eventually, my heaving subsides and I curl up on the cool tile floor, sobbing as my heart shreds to pieces. Her written words echo in my head until I slowly lose consciousness.

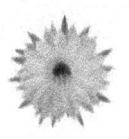

Dear Stu,
If you're reading this, I'm already gone. But don't worry, I'm finally free.
You were the greatest light in my life when all I knew was darkness. For that, I thank you. I know you won't understand why I had to do this, but just know, I probably would have done it much sooner had it not been for you.
I'm sorry I got so mad at you. I was scared, exposed, and felt all too vulnerable. So, I did what I do best; I pushed you away no matter how much it hurt.
I want you to know, it wasn't you. I'm just too jacked up. I did what I needed to do for me. I hope one day you can forgive me.
Until then, know this; I love you, Stu; with every beat of my crappy, dark, shattered heart. The thought of living without you is so painful. But, having to live with the memories of my past is unbearable.
I hope you find happiness, Stu. Even though I always knew it wouldn't be with me. You deserve someone as wonderful, kind, and awesome as you are. Never settle for less.
Always and forever yours,
Beatrice

P.S. I know you live with your friends but, in case you need more space, my lawyer should be contacting you soon. My 10-acre property is all yours now. Enjoy it!
For me.

A NOTE FROM THE AUTHOR

Woah, there. Are you ok? Do you need a tissue? I'm sorry if the ending was a bit much, but I promise it will be worth it in the end.

Thank you so much for reading the first book of the Not-So Childish Games Duet! I have totally fallen in love with the guys and I hope you have, too.

Also, a huge shout-out to my bestie, editor, and beta reader, Kayla! You are forking amazing and I love having you in my life!

Follow me on Facebook and TikTok for information about upcoming books and overall ridiculousness.
Facebook: https://www.facebook.com/groups/1422660571980693/
TikTok: https://www.tiktok.com/@triswynterswrites
Instagram:

TRISWYNTERSWRITES

ALSO BY TRIS WYNTERS

The Consumed Series

DARK REVERSE HAREM/POLYAMOROUS ROMANCE

See Me

Save Me

Free Me

Not-So Childish Games Duet

DARK REVERSE HAREM/POLYAMOROUS ROMANCE

Hide, Don't Seek

Coming Soon:

Tag, We're It